I met Timothy Dodd in 2013 while we were both attending the University of Texas El Paso's MFA writing program. It was my first semester and my first fiction workshop, and I was looking to make connections. I'd been walking through a kind of literary desert, so when I found a West Virginian on the class message board, I had to ask him if he'd read the stories of Breece Pancake. He had, of course, and my first real literary friendship was kindled on the hillside of Breece's fine work.

Of course, we talked about other writers we loved. I sold him on Larry Brown and Barry Hannah, and he recommended Ann Pancake and Clarice Lispector to me. As the years rolled on, I read much of Dodd's work, and I realized that to call Timothy Dodd a West Virginia writer, or an Appalachian writer, or a Southern Writer was to do him an injustice. It would be like calling Dylan Thomas a Welsh poet.

In stories like "Mannequins" and "Relocation" Dodd begins on the surface but takes the reader deep down. Appalachian, yes, but there's a wider lens as well. At the same time the sense of place and the stamp of authenticity never disappears: look into "Upstairs" or 'Fissures" or "Tunnel," the very first story he wrote, as I recall.

With Dodd, there is no self-conscious attempt to insert cultural landmarks or guideposts in the work, because the work, by being his, is already everything it needs to be. As readers, we arrive at what his stories are naturally, and not as tourists to his tour guide. No, Dodd is a friendly local, someone who understands what his fellow literary travelers really seek: authenticity and a peculiar sensibility that strike a nerve through vivid characterization and telling conflict of a particular place and time.

—Steve Lambert, author of *Heat Seekers*

BOTTOM DOG PRESS

HURON, OHIO

FISSURES,
AND OTHER STORIES

TIMOTHY DODD

CONTEMPORARY APPALACHIAN WRITING
BOTTOM DOG PRESS
HURON, OHIO

CREDITS:
General Editor: Larry Smith
Cover & Layout Design: Susanna Sharp-Schwacke
Cover Art: Timothy Dodd, *Faith and Faithlessness*
Author Photo: Aiggee Patilan

ACKNOWLEDGEMENTS

"Baptism" in *The William & Mary Review*; "Burials" in *Anthology
of Appalachian Writers*; "Blue Bloke" in *Coe Review*; "Just Like It
Used to Be" in *Owen Wister Review*; "Fissures" in *Metal Scratches*;
"Upstairs" in *Dewpoint Literary Journal*; "Relocation" in *Wraparound
South*; "Greener Ground" as "Verdant Grounds" in *Appalachian
Story*; "Mannequins" in *Main Street Rag*; "Through the Hollow"
in *saltfront*; "Sleepwalkers" in *Sand Hill Review*; "Postcards" in
Perceptions; "By Warlock's Design" in *The Rampallian*; "When We
Settle" in *You Are Here*.

TABLE OF CONTENTS

Something in you must die before you can possess and command.
—Sherwood Anderson, "Brother Death"

I looked for my hat, which was in a different place each time I reached for it: I couldn't get hold of it or leave.
—Felisberto Hernandez, "The Two Stories"

Baptism

The cold water ran off Estelle's body as they lifted her, falling back into the river like the cupfuls of bathwater she once poured over Jaimee. Estelle wiped her face with both hands and opened her eyes to a glaring sun, then a thick line of birch and elm along the riverbank—a streak of blurred green. Hugh Krone's voice boomed as he quoted scripture. Estelle pinched her nose and closed her eyes as the pastor's chubby hands led her down for a second submersion.

Fifteen minutes earlier she had left the small, whitewashed church and walked the short path down to the Bluestone River. The small congregation of Lorton Lick Independent Baptist Church surrounded her, singing hymns. Her husband James wouldn't have believed she had attended church services for the past two months, but where else could she turn for help once his life insurance money ran out? Before his mining accident, he wouldn't have believed she'd start a hot dog stand at the mouth of the hollow either, or place ads in the paper offering house cleaning, car washing, and lawn work. Nor would he have allowed her to sell their house because the monthly payments were too high. Yet she did all those things. She even tried a new man. Sheldon Dudley. But she was tired and there was no love on her part, no energy, and Sheldon lost interest after a month.

Each month grew more difficult financially. Even their small, two-bedroom apartment cost too much, and Estelle fell behind on the rent and had to pay late fees. Rebecca grew out of her clothes and so needed new ones each year. Jaimee turned fourteen and asked for new shoes, a Walkman, and weekly stipend for spending money. Estelle tried to generate new income, but had to tell her eldest daughter there was only money enough for necessities.

Reverend Krone and his scrawny assistant, Coleman Parr, lowered her again, their voices muted as they held Estelle for a moment under the water. She barely heard them, like when James used to cheer for her at volleyball games in Montcalm High School's gymnasium. More than Hugh Krone, Estelle heard her mother speaking.

"If you marry that man and follow him to Bluefield, it'll be the end of our property. I know it. Once you all put me in the dirt, you'll sell it off before I can even get comfortable down there."

"Can't live in the past, Mom. Don't expect me to stay here just because Gene and Tammy didn't. Even if I am your last option."

"No, I can't. You're right about that. You all are going to do what you want to do. Just remember, someday you might wish you had kept this place. But I guess whoever you sell this land to will be stuck with me. Takes an awful long time for bones to disintegrate. Especially mine."

"Wish you'd quit talking like that, Mother. You're always so morbid."

"Ain't nothing morbid about dying. Better dead than forsaken."

The men walked Estelle back to the riverbank, her eyes tearing as the congregation sang "How Great Thou Art." A churchwoman handed her two towels, one to dry her hair and the other to wrap around her shoulders. *I see the stars, I hear the rolling thunder. Thy power throughout the universe displayed.* Estelle shook their hands, one by one. She was Sister Wickline now, praise God, but wet and cold once the euphoria wore off.

The church members sounded like a flock of sparrows, chattering and whistling and chirping as they paraded happily back to the church. Hugh Krone, trudging down the path in sopping khakis and white t-shirt, accepted congratulations for winning another soul, his grinning face looking much younger than his forty-three years.

Estelle thought of her husband again. James never grinned like Hugh Krone. James never looked young. James walked under the earth for two decades digging out the dark rock.

She had needed Pastor Krone's enthusiasm.

"Don't you worry, Estelle," he said during one of his Thursday evening visits to her home before she got saved,

Coleman Parr at his side. "You can't expect to fix all this yourself. You have to believe in Him. Matthew 11:28 says, 'Come unto me, all ye that labour and are heavy laden, and I will give you rest.' Not to mention the church could probably find some way to help you out a little financially. Maybe we can help you find a better job than the one you've got at Fas Chek."

Estelle liked the sound of that, wondered if he could find her a position at Gasco where he worked as an operations supervisor.

Jaimee, her eldest daughter, brought them coffee on those nights, alongside oatmeal raisin cookies or warm cornbread, and pretended she was a waitress working for tips. No one had visited their home much after her father died, and she used the pastor's visit as an excuse to fix herself up and put on her favorite Sasson jeans.

"You ought to be with us too, young lady," Reverend Krone said to Estelle's daughter, chewing his second cookie. He looked at her quite a bit longer, but Jaimee didn't say anything until he asked about her friends, cheerleading, and the honor roll. When they prayed each week to conclude their visit, the pastor asked that they form a circle to hold hands. Each time he made sure he got a hold of Jaimee's.

Estelle had walked down an empty Main Street on a chilly Tuesday evening. First Community Bank and Family Dollar, the only two businesses still in town, had closed for the day. Moments after deciding it couldn't hurt to attend Pastor Krone's church, she stopped in front of Gandee's Shoe Shop. Out of business for over a generation, its faded "OPEN" sign still hung crookedly on the door amidst cobwebs. Estelle whispered her husband's name, remembering when they had visited the store together as young adults. She told James she didn't want her life, or Rebecca and Jaimee's lives, turning into those darkened interiors of abandoned buildings. There was no farm for going back. There was no land to sustain them. Like so many others, they had bet on the highway to take them some place better. Now the highway between her family's farm and Bluefield gave them little more than Burger Kings and 7-11s, Slurpees and lottery tickets, all glued together in a wild rush by Amoco and Exxon.

A couple of weeks later, one Sunday morning in March, Estelle quietly entered Lorton Lick. Unsure what to expect, she warmed when the parishioners smiled and welcomed her, said more to her in an hour than they had said to her in a decade. On a Wednesday night a month later, with far fewer people in attendance, she walked to the altar weeping and bowed down. Linda Archibald and Elma Boyd cried with her until their tears turned to happiness, for one of the lost had returned home to the flock.

Estelle was washing dishes when the doorbell rang on the evening after she got saved. Hugh Krone and Coleman Parr stood waiting on the porch, Bibles tucked against their chests.

"Evening, Pastor. Guess I didn't expect you all this week." A smell of strong cologne wafted into the house.

"Well, you're not the only one in this household who needs the Lord, Sister Wickline."

And every Thursday they kept coming, even after the weather warmed up and Estelle was baptized.

"She's just a girl still, Pastor Krone," Estelle said one evening as she let them inside the house.

"Sometimes Mommy is the last to know," Pastor Krone replied. "God forbid she was to die tomorrow. Where would her soul go? Fourteen years old ain't as young as you think. If you need any evidence, I can give it to you."

Estelle didn't know the answer to his question. "I understand, Pastor Krone. She's upstairs doing her algebra homework now. Rebecca, go up and tell your big sister to come down a minute."

"No, no. No reason to interrupt her from her studies," Pastor Krone said. "I'll just go on up myself if that's all right." He started up the narrow flight of stairs, his large frame surprisingly supple. "I want to remind her we expect to see her this Sunday. Shouldn't take long."

"Second door on your right, Reverend Krone," Estelle called.

"I'll just stay here on the couch," Coleman Parr declared, hands on his knees.

"That'd be fine, Brother Parr," Estelle said as she excused herself to the kitchen with Rebecca following.

Ten minutes later they came out with a pot of black tea and a tray of cheese and crackers alongside some raw vegetables. Estelle poured a steaming cup for the deacon as he reached for celery and sharp cheddar.

"Rebecca, go up and tell the preacher he's got a cup of hot tea waiting on him."

Rebecca ran up the stairs to inform her sister, found the bedroom door closed and locked. She knocked three times. The bedsprings from inside Jaimee's room squeaked and Hugh Krone finally opened the door, said they'd be right down.

The pastor came down a few minutes later, smiling, his cheeks ruddy and his big bear frame making the stairs creak. "Did you say tea or coffee?"

"Tea, Pastor Krone."

"All right, then," he said, sitting down next to Deacon Parr. "Your daughter and I had a good talk, Sister Wickline. She had some questions, but we're making headway. She knows what's expected. I'll leave it in your hands to make sure she starts coming on a regular basis. No more of this on-a-week, off-a-week stuff."

Four months after her own baptism, Estelle watched with pride as Pastor Krone and Coleman Parr led Jaimee out into the river where she herself had been led.

A few short months earlier, Jaimee gave her mother excuses to avoid attending church; one Friday evening she even said she didn't want to go at all anymore. But Estelle persisted, made her go, and Jaimee followed her mother's orders. Jaimee never talked much at church, even to the girls her own age when the congregation got together for a dinner or picnic and softball. Then one Sunday night Hugh Krone found Estelle and her daughter lingering in their pew after the service, the girl in tears. Pastor Krone asked if she wanted to give her life to the Lord. Jaimee moved her head ever so slightly—Estelle thinking nothing of it, but Pastor Krone shouted, "Praise God!"

They were now in the water above their knees and Pastor Krone stopped at the same spot in the river where he had baptized Estelle. The two men let go of the girl's hands, and Jaimee pushed a strip of her long, blonde hair back over her ear as she peered into the water.

Estelle couldn't see her daughter's face, but admired the white cotton dress, a gift she had given her on her birthday a few weeks earlier. Jaimee had said she liked the dress, but didn't show the excitement Estelle expected. Estelle marked it up to maturity, to growing up. Now she couldn't help but notice her daughter's fine figure as the breeze tightened the dress around her body.

Hugh Krone and Coleman Parr each put one hand on Jaimee's back while their other hands tightened a grip around the teen's upper arms. Pastor Krone shouted the words, "I baptize you in the name of the Father, the Son, and the Holy Ghost," and they laid Jaimee down, under the water. She came up crying and shivering, but the men said nothing, preparing to put her under a second time.

Estelle fidgeted at the river's edge. Jaimee had never feared water, even volunteered as a lifeguard at the community swimming pool. Estelle squinted to look more closely, then closed her eyes. The trees along the opposite riverbank looked plastic, and the river water turned to an iron-fused, rusty orange. When she opened her eyes, Hugh Krone had never appeared so ugly, his eyes bulging and his head shaped like a cinderblock. In the sunlight, his dyed, slick-backed hair looked like pyrite. And Estelle knew why his eyes popped out: the water had soaked Jaimee's dress, revealing the shape of her youthful breasts.

Estelle stepped into the water, one hand in the air and the other covering her mouth. She wanted to wade out into the river to reach her daughter, but a shaken Jaimee neared the bank as Pastor Krone and Brother Coleman paraded her back, holding her tightly by the arms.

At the riverbank Jaimee balled up and wilted in Estelle's arms. The congregation quieted and looked on with confused faces. "What happened, Pastor Krone?" one of the parishioners called out.

"Oh, I believe she just got a little water in her lungs. There's a lot of water out there you know. Praise God, that's all right! The Kingdom of the Lord is hers!"

As Estelle embraced her daughter, something hard rubbed against her stomach. She reached down to Jaimee's waist, and through her dress and underwear she felt the old, leather knife and pouch that James had used during deer season. Estelle looked back at Pastor Krone.

A few members of the congregation stepped forward to congratulate Jaimee, but Estelle motioned them off with her hand. Pastor Krone walked over and laid his hand on Estelle's shoulder. "Everything all right, Sister Wickline?"

14

"I'm sure, Pastor, that something more than a little water in the lungs happened to my daughter out there."

"Well I don't know what it could be, Sister. Maybe she just needs a little space and time?"

"Yes. I'd say so."

"All right, then." Pastor Krone turned to the members of his church. "Brothers and Sisters, Jaimee isn't feeling too well right now and Sister Wickline thinks it best if we give them a little breathing space for the moment. If you'd be so kind, please make your way back to the church and we'll reconvene again tomorrow morning for our usual Sunday morning service. Drive safely and God bless."

The congregation departed, leaving Hugh Krone and Coleman Parr standing on the path next to the riverbank, a few feet from Estelle and Jaimee.

"Sister Wickline, would you all want me to bring you any extra towels?"

Estelle didn't answer.

"Well, I hope everything turns out okay. Whatever it is, I know the Lord can work it out. Praise God, Jaimee's born-again." He paused. "You all have my number if you need anything."

Estelle listened as the sound of lumbering footsteps faded. Jaimee's sobbing started in again. Estelle tightened her arms around her daughter and rested her chin on the top of Jaimee's head.

Estelle thought of James as she held her daughter close. She thought of what he had told her all the years they were married, all the years he worked the mines: "Those safety regulations don't mean a thing. The company only adheres when it's good for them." She remembered the mine wagon that brought the bodies up out of the ground after the cave wall collapsed on him and his six workmates. She recalled having to point at him, claim which swollen, unrecognizable head belonged to her husband.

Jaimee didn't move from her mother's breast. Estelle clutched her daughter and looked out at the water. The land around them lay still except for the soft gurgling of the river. It could wash, but she wasn't sure if it could cleanse. She remembered her mother again, remembered a simpler time growing up when she spent the day feeding the chickens, collecting eggs, or helping her daddy pitch hay.

Then Estelle turned and looked toward the church. August's excessive heat had wilted the tall grass alongside the path so that it rose no better than a frail man tired of an unsustainable pace.

Ten minutes more passed and still Estelle didn't know what to say to Jaimee except that things would be okay. It was new territory, as James used to say some days after coming home from work, and her arms and chest were tight from holding her daughter. Estelle began to sway ever so slightly, trying to mimic the Bluestone as it rolled on. And she thought how James used to love the sounds down in the mines, especially the drops of water falling onto rock.

BURIALS

Two kernel-cleaned corncobs land inside the shaded pen with a hollow sound, as lifeless as the $2.99 plastic guns Uncle Jack buys at McCrory's for Tyler. The fattened, isolated sow moves its snout, angles its jaws, and laps them up. Leaning over the fence, I toss in a couple of bruised, yellow apples picked off the ground—sweetness before tomorrow's knife. No one told me the animal shouldn't eat the day before it's slaughtered.

I wipe the fruits' sour stickiness onto my jeans and kick the hard ground in front of the pen with the toe of my Converse, chipping the dirt. My eyes rise to the soft curves of the ridgeline covered by American beech and black birch. From a distance the hills never look far away, running up and down like a kid under the sky's fluffy white beards. I breathe in the air of a rich and full-bodied land—like inhaling a concentrated smell after opening a sealed can, or a closet door closed for the longest time. There's the scent of mountain laurel and rotten apples, of livestock, but there's something more as well, something missing in town.

I know Grandmother will never leave. The soil is in her pores, under her fingernails, between the folds of her skin. She'd rather be worn by the earth than engines and telephones.

I walk out past the cattle pastures where she still keeps a dozen head. On a small clearing in the woods our family headstones pop out of the ground like spring flowers, crooked and leaning. I move over the lumpy ground, tiptoeing between graves and reading the names on the tombs: Jeremy Maupin, Silas Maupin, Evelyn Sizemore. The oldest writing has worn away with memories, leaving grave markers that look like rocks shaped more by erosion than a human hand. Without Grandmother, all the names would be lost; plucked from history like a shrew by a red-tailed hawk. Once we lay her down next to Grandfather, her body will be the last stored here. Then the cemetery itself will start to die, will drift back into the mountains with wood pewee and wren song.

Jimmy is in the chicken coop cleaning out the manure when I get back. I walk slowly and nod my head at him a few times, but can't get his attention. Uncle Jack has parked his Subaru on the bank, probably lamenting that there's no parking lot.

"Where you been?" Mom asks when I get inside the house. She's helping Grandmother set the table.

"Out with the hogs," I say, eyeing the bacon and eggs, homemade apple butter, and coffee.

Mom sees the briars stuck in my flannel shirt and the limestone dust from the tombs on my palms, but only Grandmother knows where I've gone. No one else thinks anyone would go to the cemetery except out of obligation. Grandmother stops to look at me, a plate of biscuits in her hands, wearing one of her best dresses, cream-colored with bright pink flowers. I see the tick-tick-tick of her mind, the sound of a clock in an empty room, the time that has passed her. But she knows plenty that the rest of us don't.

"Where's Uncle Jack and Aunt Tammy?" I ask. Their kids are kicking around in the other room with Joanna.

"They just got here, Zach," Uncle Roland says with one leg half-stretched out across the low, black sofa. "They're in the bathroom now. You know how it takes them a good, long while to freshen up, as they say. Apparently, a lot gets dirtied between here and Gaithersburg."

"Both of them in there?"

"I reckon."

Mom puts out a two liter of Coca-Cola, and Grandmother lays down a big pot of fried potatoes.

"Zachary, go and wash up and get your sister and cousins. And tell Jack and Tammy the table's ready," Mom says. "Come on, Roland. It's ready."

Roland stands up with a lazy groan and surveys the table. "Now I don't recall ever eating bacon and eggs this late in the day."

"Roland, we do this every year to please everybody," Grandma replies.

"Don't listen to him, Mother. He's just pulling your leg."

Uncle Jack walks into the kitchen. "You look awful pretty, Mother," he says. "Don't have you a man around here, do you?" Aunt Tammy trails him, crouched behind like she's hiding.

"Leave her alone, Jack," Mother says.

"Well, now, you never know. And what's wrong with that anyway? Might do some good."

"That's a Maupin for you, ain't it, Tammy?" Roland jokes.

I leave the kitchen and walk to the bathroom, passing by the living room to tell my little sister and the cousins that it's time to eat. Uncle Jack and Aunt Tammy's overnight kits are on the bathroom sink. They've brought their own liquid soap as well: cucumber and melon with cleansing beads from Bath and Bodyworks. I reach for Grandma's homemade soap bar and turn the knob. The sulfur-smelling water runs out a light brown. I lather and rinse.

When I get back to the kitchen everyone is seated and dishing up the food except for Aunt Tammy and her two children who are standing over a cooler in the corner of the room.

"Well, you deserve a little luxury occasionally, Mother," Uncle Jack says as his wife hands a pre-made cheese and tomato sandwich to their seven-year-old daughter.

"I want an iced coffee," Tyler shouts.

"We'll get one in the morning," Aunt Tammy replies.

At the table, Grandmother has put her fork down on her plate and stopped eating. "If Janet don't want it, take it back or give it to someone else," she says.

"Be a lot easier to trim them weeds, Mother," Mom says. "All you need are some batteries and it'll keep them black snakes from coming around."

"I ain't going to use it."

"Take it back, Jack," Roland says as he fixes another biscuit. "If Mother says she ain't going to use it, she ain't going to use it."

Mouths crunch on bacon and forks clink against Fiestaware. "Are you all staying the night this year?" I ask Uncle Jack after I fill up my plate and sit down at the table.

"No, no. We've got a reservation at the Holiday Inn for two nights. Best thing we could find this year." He leans over to me and lowers his voice, "Tammy isn't pleased with it, but I don't know where else we'd stay if there's nothing in Elkins. I might just have to start coming here each year by myself."

I slice open a biscuit and spread a thick layer of Grandmother's apple butter on each half, stuff one side whole into my mouth. How much would Grandmother miss Zoe and Tyler, Aunt Tammy, if they didn't come?

19

"Well, I guess it's number fifty-nine tomorrow, Mother," Uncle Jack says loudly so Grandma hears him across the table.

She smiles. "That was four or five presidents ago."

I start to eat faster. I've heard the same conversation many times before.

"Now let's think about that," Uncle Roland says. "Reagan, Carter, Ford, Nixon, Johnson, Kennedy. Then Eisenhower, wasn't it, Jack?"

"That's right."

"That's more than four or five, Mother."

"I ain't concerned with them presidents," Grandmother says as she chews on fried potatoes. "Just wish Sarah was here. Like to see her."

"She's over on the other side of the country, Mother. You know that. She can't get in here every year. It's a long trip," Uncle Jack explains.

"Still in California, ain't she?"

"Yeah. San Francisco."

"Working with them computers?"

"Sure is. And she's doing well. Computers are today's gold."

"What you mean doing well?" Grandma asks with a glare.

"Making good money, Mother."

Grandma turns to my sister and pats her on the leg below the table. "You going to work on them computers, too?" Joanna doesn't respond, only smiles as a piece of bacon hangs from the corner of her mouth.

"Roland, are you slaughtering this afternoon or are you expecting Jimmy to do it again?" my mother asks, changing the subject.

"Don't know if I've got it in me this year," he says. "Anyway, I believe it's Jack's turn. Maybe he can surprise us all for once. What do you think, Jack? Surely you ain't going to make that skinny little orphan boy do everything around here. Just wear your red button-down so the blood won't show."

"I'll do it myself," Grandmother says.

"No, you ain't, Mother," Mom says. "Let one of the men do it."

"Ain't no men around here no more." When she gets excited and talks, her dentures clop.

"This one's going to be a sweet one, ain't it?" Roland asks.

"I figure. Been feeding it golden delicious and clabber for over a month."

I stuff another piece of bacon in my mouth with some fried potatoes, wash it down with the last of my Coke. Tyler is pouting because Aunt Tammy just told him there isn't any television this far away from home. I start fixing a second plate. "Grandma, I'm going to take a plate out to Jimmy. That okay?"

"Be fine. Give him more potatoes than eggs. He likes them better. Take him a cup of coffee, too, if you can. He's probably in the barn about now."

I finish fixing the plate, pour a cup of coffee, and head outside. I don't see Jimmy so I walk to the barn. He's inside cleaning, and he jumps a little when I call his name.

"Here, Jimmy, I brought you a plate."

He stutters his thank you and starts eating right away, a boy two years younger than me who looks middle-aged. His rough hands grip the fork awkwardly. I wonder where he's from. I wonder if his family has a cemetery laid out somewhere in the hills. Grandmother only says his parents died when he was three years old. He wouldn't know how to live in Elkins or Weston any more than I'd know how to live here with Grandmother. I want to ask him if he likes baseball, what he does in his free time, but even these things take more than a weekend. I turn and walk out of the barn so he can eat in peace, go back into the house.

After the dishes are washed, Grandmother makes a fresh pot of coffee and everyone except for Jack's kids sits around the table playing Uno. A plate of roasted peanuts and dried pumpkin seeds is passed around. Even Grandmother plays a couple of hands before quietly getting up to find Jimmy and slaughter the hog.

"Go and help her, Roland," Mom says.

"She don't want my help. Her and Jimmy know what they're doing."

I can tell that he and Uncle Jack have money riding on the games. "Even Uno?" I ask.

"You be still or you'll get me in even more trouble," he says.

Uncle Jack and his family leave an hour before sunset. Night falls fast and Joanna falls asleep on the couch. Without electricity a person gets sleepy real quickly once it's dark. Uncle Roland wants to take me outside for a drink, but I go into the bedroom. There's an extra bed for me and I put down the blankets. I lie down and feel the wires digging into my back as the bed sags towards the floor.

An hour or two later I wake up to Grandmother's raised voice in the kitchen. "I ain't going."

"Mother, we just want what's best for you. It's not that safe living out here all by your lonesome."

"That ain't my fault."

I stand up and go to the bathroom. The cold air has come in since the sun went down. I remember Dad telling how he got up at five in the morning to walk for an hour and a half in the winter cold to get to school.

"A slice of bread with a little butter or bacon grease, two if you were lucky, and a cup of chicory to warm you. That's it. Off you go."

When I return from the bathroom Uncle Roland is asking Mom how she's doing, how long she'll make it on the money he left her. I never asked Dad what it was like getting up before five to go down into the mines.

"It helps, but it ain't going to last," Mom says. "I'm working night shifts at the Amoco, and Zachary's on at Go-Mart. I think they're going to hire him for the Corbett 13 Mine though. Mr. Ramsey promised me anyway."

I still can't tell her I can't do it, can't convince myself to scrape innards from a blasted mountain. I'm tempted to come back and live here with Grandmother, get away from the blacktop and candy bars and gasoline, but I'd be no use. And when she dies—could be any year people say—only weeds and snakes will inherit the place.

The next morning I'm up by sunrise. I step into the kitchen where Grandmother is standing alone.

"Happy Birthday, Grandma."

She thanks me. "Breakfast'll be ready in just a minute."

"Anything I can do to help out?"

"No, no. Sit down, Zachary. Eat a little breakfast with me and then I've got to go and get Jimmy to get the meat ready. Sleep okay?"

"Fine, Grandma." I sit down and wait quietly. Neither of us are the best friends of chitchat.

She puts the leftover potatoes on the table with a couple of hard-boiled eggs and some bread and butter. "Looking forward to that fresh pork today?"

"Sure," I say. "Don't get meat like that in town."

She smiles. "Not many more birthdays left in me, Zachary."

"Don't talk like that, Grandma. I expect you'll hit a hundred."

"Now don't tell me that." She sits down at the table across from me with her coffee. "I ain't living my last days in an old age home or the hospital neither. They better believe that."

"Noah Maupin lived to be 103."

Grandma repeats the name. "You were out to the cemetery yesterday. Boy, he was a strong man, Zachary. Had a light grey beard that looked as soft as cotton. I was twelve years old when he died. He kept them bees and people used to love his clover honey. I remember one time he gave me a jar of it, told me to take it home to Mother. I must have been around eight years old and didn't know what it was. Before I could get home I got the lid off somehow to try it. Got it all over the outside of the jar, all over my hands. Even tried to wipe it off on my dress. Mother was none too pleased with me."

I sit quietly and listen, waiting for the right time to respond.

"Well, what are we going to do? By the way, did anyone ever take you down over the hill to the house where your mother grew up?"

"No. Never knew about it."

"Have Roland take you down there when he gets up. He ought to be able to find it. We moved out of it about twenty years ago or so. The roof's gone and plants and ferns and young trees are growing all around last I saw it. I figure by now they're growing inside it too—where your mother and uncles used to crawl around. It don't take long. No, sir. Nothing wrong with this land."

I dip an egg in salt and bite off half, down into the yolk. I can't explain it, but it tastes different than supermarket eggs.

"Do your grandmother one favor, Zachary. Make sure your mother puts me in that cemetery, you hear? I told her I don't want to go no place else. I don't care if no one's around to care for it. Put me there and I've done my part. What the rest of them want to do is up to them."

"Don't worry, Grandma. I know Mom will do it how you want."

"I ain't so sure. You just keep on her about it for me., you hear?"

I wait for more words, but Grandmother says nothing more. She finishes her meager breakfast quickly, sets her cup and plate in the sink, and heads outside.

Uncle Jack and his family return around noon. I ask Uncle Roland mid-morning if he'll take me to see the old Maupin family house. He says he will, but never does.

By mid-afternoon the family is feasting. I get a plate full of pork, potato salad, and half runners cooked in lard. The pork is tender and tangy, and I eat fast. I fix a second plate for myself, then a third that I take out to Jimmy.

After I drop off his food, while the family is talking and finally tiring from stuffing themselves, I walk back to the cemetery again. I sit down and watch the sunlight bounce off the granite and limestone. Shapes roll off the tombstones. They float into the mountains or just disappear. I try to visualize Noah Maupin and the others. For every woman's name I see on a grave, I think of Grandma. I hear her voice, old and heated, as if I'm imagining words that already passed on. Then I think of Dad and how he's buried another way, the rock crashing down on him, his body unrecoverable. I remember him during mornings before work: his pale skin in his white t-shirt and Fruit of the Looms, his beady eyes quiet and vacant.

Tomorrow morning, on our drive home, I'll bring up Grandma's wishes to Mom. I might tell her that if anything happens to me I'd like to be buried here too. Then I've got to tell her I can't do the work Dad once did. I can't go down in those mines, can't pick and scalp and blow up the land that's all we've got to take us in again when we die.

Back at the house over an hour later the family is still outside, sitting around the wood table. The smell of roasted pork hangs in the air. When I step onto the property clearing, Grandma is looking straight at me. When I get closer I see she's smiling. Not because it's her birthday or Uncle Roland has made them laugh. Not because the pork is delicious or because she's surrounded by visiting family, but because she sees me coming, and knows she'll have her resting place.

BLUE BLOKE

They're shooting again. So little Cory's screaming again.

"Honey, go put something on for him," Shirley says.

I walk to the living room. On the ground beside the entertainment center I find a disc out of its case. I pick it up and slam Grover's face into the DVD player, turn up the volume.

Every Saturday now we keep turning the volume louder and louder just to drown out their pow-pow-pow. And after Grover, comes Big Bird. Then Elmo. Then Kermit. Then repeat. Until mid-afternoon. By then my mind feels like a wrecked Kings Island ride. Some weekends I feel like we'll still be watching these shows when Cory's a grown man. Other weekends I have to up and leave for a beer down at Squeaky's.

I never anticipated this problem when we moved out to this rural, upper middle-class housing development three years ago, but it's a weekend retreat for them; that's what it is. Since the "For Sale" sign was taken down at the end of October, they've come from town every Friday evening, even Christmas, to stay up on the ridge. Each Saturday morning they walk down the hillside, three or four men with beagles and twelve-gauges, hunting rabbits in the thickets across their five acres behind my home. No need to check with the police or the church: it's not illegal and there's no sin. And with little to no snow on the ground, this winter hasn't helped.

They start shooting even before we're out of bed, often just when I begin to enjoy the warmth of my wife and the new down comforter from Kaufmann's. Even if by some small chance I don't hear the first shot, Rocky hears it and wakes us up anyway with his barking. By now I'm used to getting up at the first crack. I go downstairs and pace around, brew the Maxwell House. I used to look forward every week to those couple extra hours of sleep on the weekend, but they don't exist anymore. The gunshots rattle me. They rattle me even before they reach my ears. I go to bed thinking about them, and after I fall asleep, deep in the night, there's still some part of me waiting on them. Shirley finally told me, "Honey, come Fridays you toss around in bed now like a dying fish."

With Grover jabbering at full blast, I go back into the kitchen. They're standing at my property line this minute. Fifteen yards from my living room window as Shirley sets biscuits and apple butter from the farmer's market on the kitchen table. I can see the burlap bags they carry over their shoulders so clearly that I could count how many rabbits are inside. Barrels are pointed at the ground as their splotchy dogs sniff near the piles of brush. I figure the dogs are close enough to smell the bacon frying on our stove. Even when they're on the far side of their property I can see the men's orange hunting vests through the barren trees. I watch as they lead their hounds up over the knoll, out of view, then circle back again.

"You want any hot sauce this morning?" Shirley asks after she calms Cory down, deciding not to carry him into the living room. I barely hear her over the "Waiter, there's a fly in my soup" skit. I learned to put hot sauce on my scrambled eggs from a Mexican fellow who I was stationed with at Fort Bragg, and I don't know why Shirley even bothers asking anymore. That's the only way I can eat them.

Cory is in his highchair. He was content sucking his pacifier, ready for his bottle of milk, until the shots started up again. Shirley herself is shaking now since they're so close. I figure half of her shakes are on account of me, the others are for Cory. It's like when we had bed bugs in the barracks. We didn't fear the bites so much as knowing that we were surrounded and incapable. It's the anticipation, the helplessness, I guess—the knowing that your assault rifles won't help you a damn.

"You want more coffee?" she asks before stting down to feed our boy.

But then there's another loud pop. Then three more. The hunters' hounds start howling, and Rocky walks over and curls up in the corner, not knowing what to make of things anymore. Cory's mouth wrinkles after the first crack, and he's bawling again after the second shot even though Shirley picks him up and swings him onto her shoulder. I jump up from my chair, apple butter falling from a biscuit onto my hand. That's it, I tell myself. I can't live like this every weekend for another two months. Hell, they might even start shooting possums in March.

Thursday after work I drive up on the ridge to make sure the men haven't arrived for an early weekend. Then I continue home and talk Shirley into taking Cory with her to the supermarket for the pasta and red peppers I conveniently forgot. After she leaves, I grab two industrial grade plastic bags from the closet where I've stored the box of Havoc pellets. I put on my Caterpillar boots and leave through the patio door.

Only two months ago, the second weekend they hunted, I called from the back porch and walked out to talk to them. There were three of them that weekend, all with fluorescent orange jackets, cheap-ass twelve-gauges, fatigues, brown boots, and hunting caps. Around fifty years old. Overweight. Moustaches. I couldn't tell them apart.

"It's my property and I've got a right to hunt on it," one of the men said. "Go ahead and call your sheriff; I'd be glad to show off my permit. You and your family ain't outside during the wintertime anyway."

I didn't say much. They could care less if they wake me up early or frighten my family and rile my dog. I thought about telling them I was in the 82nd Airborne Division and fought in the Iraq War, or that I spent two years at Camp Bravo in Basra. But they'd either take that as a threat or a lie, not a simple call for some respect. Then I thought about ripping the pitiful guts out of each of their potbellies. Instead I just turned and walked back to the house, worried I might go and pick up my AR-15. It's a short space for me between folding and snapping.

Two weekends later, the weekend after Thanksgiving, a party of six trampled the woods. It was a warm Saturday and I took my speakers out onto the back porch, cranked up some Thin Lizzy and Zeppelin just to show them things work both ways. One of the hunters came up to the porch and said the music made it impossible to hunt.

"I've got a right to listen to my music, don't I?"

"Yeah. At a reasonable volume, you do."

"How about your gunshots? They at a reasonable volume? Ask my one-year-old son if they're a reasonable volume."

"Now that's different. And we ain't but using twelve-gauges anyway." The man paused and then lowered his voice. "But we got things a lot more powerful than them if need be."

"Get off my property."

I thought of turning the music up to the point it wouldn't even sound like music, but I knew Shirley could already hear it inside the house and it made her almost as uncomfortable as the gunshots. Ten minutes later a county police officer showed up and told me I had to turn the music down; I was disturbing the peace. I followed Officer Scruggs' instructions and went back inside the house. The next evening, after we got home from shopping, I went to mow the backyard before dark and saw they had busted my attic window.

I stop in the garage to put on a pair of latex gloves and grab a small shovel, then walk through the backyard, into the woods. I've been edgy all week, and Shirley and I argued three times, all about ridiculous stuff like how to hang the hand towel on the rack after washing. I walk to the first spot where I found cropped grass and rabbit droppings earlier in the week, where I've placed Havoc each evening since Monday when I get home from work, putting it down just before the rabbits come out to feed. The pellets are gone now, just like the food I put out the week before to acclimate them.

A carcass lies near the light walking trail that the hunters have made. There's no smell and few insects; a recent death. No external bleeding from the Havoc either. I open one of the plastic bags, pick up the rabbit by its back legs, and toss it in—a complete waste that it's not meat for humans or other animals, not even useable for fur.

There's no Havoc left for the men to find at the second place either, but there are two dead rabbits in the brush about ten yards from each other. They stink and have been picked at and eaten. I set the open bag on the ground, pick up the carcasses with the shovel, and dump them inside. Three more are dead in the area of the third and final feeding area. I throw sticks at the bodies to scatter the insects, and dump them in the bag with the rest. I toss my gloves into the bag and tie it before heading back through the woods toward home.

In the garage I fill a bucket with water and set the shovel inside it to wash later. I walk to the driveway, open the passenger door to my Silverado, and put the bag of dead rabbits on the floor.

On the five-minute drive to Arby's I think about what will happen on Saturday when the men enter the woods. Let them hunt. If they find more dead rabbits, maybe they might guess what I've done. If they find live ones, let them shoot. Let them eat rabbit stew and give their dogs the innards and bones. Let them swallow the poison and let the doctors figure it out.

I pull into Arby's and drive around back to their giant, green garbage bin, get out of the car to deposit the poisoned carcasses. The bin is mostly empty and the bag hits the bottom with a metallic thud. Nothing more to do but wait for the men, wait for Saturday to come.

But when I arrive home Cory's crying and Shirley's yelling. Bright green Havoc pellets litter the entryway in front of the closet. Rocky lies on the kitchen floor, wagging his tail and licking his lips.

"You left the closet door open again."

Inside the closet Rocky has knocked the box of Havoc off the bottom shelf and pellets are lodged in crevices, stuck between boxes and bags. How many are now in my dog's stomach? One glance at him says he's had a feast.

"What is it that he's gotten into anyway, Eric? And why can't you keep the closet door closed?"

"I just forgot, Shirley," I say, quickly picking up the pellets. When I finish, I go upstairs out of earshot and call the vet. The office is already closed, so I dial the Poisoned Pet Hotline.

"You won't see symptoms for another day or two," the man tells me over the phone. "But get the dog into the vet first thing in the morning."

Downstairs Cory is still crying. Even Shirley is making a lot of noise, and the weekend hasn't even started. I walk back downstairs to take an inconspicuous look at Rocky, but Shirley jumps on me as I reach the bottom of the stairs.

"And what is it with more unpaid bills?" she yells. "Have you seen these? I know you've seen them. But you don't do nothing about it. What's wrong with you? Irresponsible is what's wrong. Sure always got enough cash for the bar and strip clubs though, don't you?"

She picks up the car keys and starts putting Cory's shoes on him.

"Where you going?"

"Mom and Dad's. I'm tired of all this. And clean your act up before you think about asking us to come back."

She slams the door behind her, Cory in her arms. On my side of the door there is complete silence, and it isn't what I'd hoped for. I hear her shoes clicking on the sidewalk. I hear the car door slam and the engine start. I look out and see two suitcases in the backseat of the vehicle. Rocky starts to whine.

The next morning I take the day off to get my old mutt to the vet. Vitamin K1 treatment is the deal. We're there by 9 o'clock, as soon as it opens, and out by 10:30. We get home and I put Rocky in his pen, then go back to bed. I don't wake until 2. That's when it really hits me that Cory and Shirley are gone, when one or both of them would be leaning on my back or twiddling my ears.

When I wake up I go downstairs, fix myself a ham and onion sandwich, covering both slices of bread with spicy mustard. I pour myself a Mountain Dew and walk over to the sofa. By this time tomorrow I figure the hunters will have made some observations and decisions. These are the remaining hours in the bunker before the potential bombs start dropping.

I turn on the TV, but there's little on but soap operas, crappy movies, and golf. I rifle through the DVDs in the entertainment center. There's *The Deer Hunter*, *Deliverance*, and *Taxi Driver*, maybe a couple others of mine. I don't need to watch any of them again. There are a few aerobics programs that Shirley bought but never uses. Everything else is for Cory. But this time none of it's for Cory, and if my platoon saw me trying to decide which Grover flick to watch, they'd wipe my ass in thirty-five different ways.

I put in the disc and sit down on the sofa, kick my feet up on the coffee table and bite into my sandwich. Grover's wearing a cape in this one. He's Super Grover. He yaps and jokes and crash lands. He talks a big game but gets nothing right. I figure Super Grover has seen his fair share of war.

I lose track of the bites I take out of my sandwich. I don't even hear Grover as he chatters on. Deep in my mind is the question of what will happen tomorrow when the men come to hunt poisoned rabbits. Behind the men peeking out from their camouflage vests, behind some kind of carcass one way or another, I see Shirley and Cory. Are they going to come back on Monday? Is a quiet house a peaceful one? Will Rocky be okay? And will Cory be around much longer to teach me this Grover guy isn't such a bad fellow?

Just Like It Used to Be

Ray heard the disconcerting buzz of hive bees surround him before a plank came down across his jaw to wake him from a light sleep. He turned his head and opened his eyes. Foul air greeted him smelling nothing like honey or spring flowers. Lola lay spread-eagle across the bed, her thick arm draped across Ray's throat, her mouth puckering as she blew wheezy lines of carbon dioxide at his head. When she inhaled, her mouth opened wide and Ray counted glittering specks of silver in multiples of three. Every night she pushed him towards the edge of the mattress where he would poke his nose down into the crevice between bed and wall.

Ray wriggled to free his skinny frame from underneath Lola's hefty body, his legs getting more tangled in the sheets. He arched his back and strained his neck to look at the alarm clock at the head of the bed, then reached out to turn it off ten minutes early; at least time for an extra cup of coffee.

He got out of bed and looked down at his wife who never got up early. *At least starting next week I can sleep late, too,* he thought. Amidst piles of magazines and clothes Ray followed a narrow trail out of the bedroom and stepped into the bathroom, its door open just enough to enter. Relying on the faint light of dawn coming through the narrow window, he sat down to urinate. With coffee on his mind he flushed and didn't wash his hands.

Boxes and cans of food that couldn't fit in the pantry covered the hallway to the kitchen, and Ray moved slowly to avoid stubbing his toe or tripping. A minute later he reached around the refrigerator to turn on a light, squinting his eyes at the twenty or more boxes of Little Debbies stacked in the corner. From noon until bedtime each day Lola ate two of the individually wrapped cakes, washing them down with whole milk or a root beer every

31

three hours, on the hour, as though they were the doctor's prescription.

Ray tried hard to ignore Lola's habits. After years of fighting her compulsions he had convinced himself it wasn't worth the hassle. *Win some, lose some*, he figured. Maybe Lola married him knowing he was a man who would not be demanding. Then again, there were no early signs he was a pushover any more than there were signs that she had an obsessive-compulsive disorder.

Ray had once blamed himself for Lola's problem. Was it a coincidence that her compulsion to collect things escalated after the doctor informed him of his infertility? He knew it hurt her deeply that they would never have any children together, but could it cause Lola to gorge and hoard?

Ray placed two slices of Piggly Wiggly white bread in the toaster. He heated water and poured it into a cup with Folgers Classic Roast and two teaspoons of sugar. He added a dash of milk to the coffee and took three gulps, then removed his toast and spread on thick globs of margarine. He took three Jimmy Dean sausage links from a package in the refrigerator and put them in the microwave. They sizzled as he arranged them on the plate next to his toast. With no place to sit down, Ray stood over the sink and ate.

After washing his plate and silverware, Ray skirted past piles of newspapers and envelopes, boxes of holiday decorations, and Fisher-Price toys, some of them never opened. He reached a small closet in the corner of the living room, the one place in the house free of clutter. Keeping it locked despite Lola's complaints, Ray opened the closet door and glanced at a honeymoon photograph hanging inside—the happy couple stood knee-deep in the Atlantic, Ray's bony arm around Lola's thin waist. He removed his pajamas and hung them on a nail on the inside of the door, then grabbed his khakis and blue oxford shirt, locked the closet, and, still in his underwear, returned to the kitchen to finish his coffee.

Back in the bathroom, Ray set his work clothes on the commode and reached for his toothbrush behind old toiletries, expired medicines, and broken gadgets. He took out toothpaste from inside the mirror cabinet, careful not to touch any other item. Past mistakes taught him that one slip of the hand might result in a cascade of falling objects, some that he'd never find again in the rubble on the floor. After brushing his teeth, Ray pulled back the shower curtain, always relieved that the piles had not yet conquered the bathtub. Stacks of soap and packets of shampoo covered the four corners of the tub, but nothing filled the basin itself. He turned on the water and let it heat before getting in to bathe.

Fifteen minutes later Ray dried himself and dressed. He poked his head inside the bedroom like he did every morning before leaving the house. "Lola, I'm off to work now," he said. He got no reply.

Outside, the warm weather had turned cooler. Ray stepped into a garage filled with lawn tools, sports equipment, and dusty boxes stacked to the ceiling. In the middle of it all sat his '87 Mazda. Ray got in and pressed the garage door opener, then backed out into the driveway. Lawn and garden equipment, two old swing sets, and a rusted refrigerator covered the front yard, its grass long dead. Ray backed into the street, closed the garage door, and pushed down on the accelerator.

For twelve years Ray had managed the Dollar Me store in Pinch, but its stacks of merchandise never reminded him of home. At the store, Ray not only managed employees, customer complaints, and inventory, but also helped arrange the shelves, keeping each section organized and displayed in its correct location. Aisles were clean and free of clutter. When Lola blamed him on occasion for their messy home, Ray thought of his neat Dollar Me store.

Ray had great success as the store's first manager. His store expanded three times during the strong economy and was no longer a mini-branch. He even won awards in both sales and customer service, and Dollar Me paid him to join other award winners at meetings in Nashville, Lexington, and Jacksonville. When the company rewarded him with a five-day trip for two to Cancun, he and Lola rolled in the sand together and ate at buffets until they felt sick.

But in the last two years the economy grew lean and business at his store declined. With diminishing sales his number of employees also dwindled. From a peak of six full-time and eight part-time workers, the branch now employed only Ray and three part-time staff. The worst news came two weeks ago when the regional manager informed Ray that Dollar Me had decided to close his store.

"What about my job?" Ray had asked his regional manager.

"I'm real sorry, Ray. I'm going to have to lay you off. But it's only temporary. You're too good a man to lose. I'll find you another location in a month or two. Just can't promise you it'll be managerial."

Ray pulled into the Dollar Me parking lot and got out of his car. He walked to the front door, keys in hand and the "Grand Closing" sign waving in front of the store's dark interior. He unlocked the door, deactivated the alarm, and looked down the aisles filled with Q-tips, little bags of dog treats, plastic ice trays, off-brand toilet paper. Ray bit his lip and then hung his head. Friday would be his last day. Each time he entered the store now, it hit him; he was losing that comfort he felt at calling something his own. With no need to slash prices or revamp the store for a going-out-of-business sale, there was not much work to take Ray's mind off the layoff. There were few customers and no need to manage staff or order more inventory.

But look on the bright side, he told himself. *Even though it would be tight financially, who minded a month or two off?* He could get some things done that he never had time to do: take in a few Alley Cat baseball games, work in his shed, maybe even clean up the house. Unfortunately, he had not broken the news to Lola yet. He knew he had to do it, but each time he thought about it, his teeth chattered and he picked the skin around his fingernails.

Ray walked through the store to his office in the back—he had to tell Lola today. He'd go home right after closing and tell her just the way Mr. Slocum told him. He opened the door to his office and sat down at his desk, scanning the room and looking at his computer. Clean, organized, and comfortable. Then he looked up at the ceiling and stroked his brow. *What would Lola say?*

Little balls of skin sat on the dashboard when Ray returned home that evening. He rolled another one and flicked it onto the passenger's seat, then pulled the garage door opener out of the glove compartment. After parking the car, Ray tried to enter the house quietly, but Lola was standing in the kitchen, washing her hands at the sink. Ray's own hands were clammy.

Lola glanced over her shoulder. "Honey, I didn't know if you were bringing back Wendy's or you wanted me to cook some chili," she said over the running water.

Ray recalled neither option, but it was too late now to prepare chili. He would have to go back out for fast food or else settle for a sandwich.

"Listen, dear," he started, then stopped and picked at a small scab on his forehead.

Lola shut off the water and turned around. "Ray, what's bugging you? Your eye's twitching."

"Look, Lola," Ray began again, "I don't mind going out and picking up something for us, but, well, it might be the last time we're eating out for the next month or two."

Lola walked slowly to her husband, her neck stuck out to look at him as if a moth crawled on his upper lip. Ray put his hands in his pockets like a third-grader waiting for a teenager to come and take his milk money.

"All right. Just say what you need to say, Ray Feasley. There's more to this story, so out with it."

"I know, dear, I...well...you see, I don't know how to put it to you, but..."

"Oh, Ray, stop talking like you got a wad of fudge in your mouth. A boy could have told his mama that his girlfriend's pregnant eight times already."

Ray walked over and gripped the sink counter. "Things haven't been going real strong at Dollar Me lately, what with the bad economy and all. And, well, the truth is they're closing the store, and I've been laid off for a month or two." Ray's eye twitched faster as he stared down at the drain.

"Laid off? Oh, Ray, they can't do that. You've worked that job for twelve fucking years."

"Now don't get all excited, honey. Mr. Slocum says it's just temporary and that he'll find me another spot. I just have to wait a month or two until something opens up."

"Opens up? Ray, you're so damn gullible. Their mouths are telling you about opening up while their hands are busy closing the store you've built. That's exactly how these people get you. You don't realize you might never set foot in another Dollar Me as long as you live unless it's to buy some of that cheap cologne you like." Lola stopped to take a deep breath. Her face had turned pale and she put her hand on her chest. "Oh, Ray, you're giving me those palpitations." She looked up again, stared at him in the eyes. "How long have you known they were planning to do this?"

Ray's grip on the counter tightened again.

"Are you ever going to learn how to stand up for yourself? Now what's the number of that Snocum?" Lola continued. "If

35

someone don't stand up for you we'll be eating out of dog bowls before we know it. Lord knows what'll be inside of them."

Ray felt his blood turn to fire at the thought of Lola contacting Mr. Slocum. He jumped at her. "Now Lola, don't rush to any conclusions and do something rash. Things'll work out. We just have to watch our money a little more closely for a month or so. That's all." He knew his argument wasn't holding any water.

"Ray, I don't think you understand. You seem more worried about telling me the news than you are worried about the news itself. Seems like you kind of even like the idea. Like you knew about this for a while and didn't tell me." She glared at Ray and stepped forward, waiting for his nerves to give him away.

"Honey, Mr. Slocum just told me yesterday," he lied. "We'll be all right, and I could do for a little break to tell you the truth. I've put a lot of hours into that store."

"Damn straight you put a lot of hours into that store. And now you're just going to let them take it from you? I'm not putting up with this. I can't. And you're crazy if you think you can hang around here for two months. You'll be sadder-looking than a deformed Basset Hound. Now give me Snocum's number."

"Lola, I don't have his number with me," Ray lied again, raising his voice. If Lola called his boss in one of her fits it could easily destroy his good reputation in minutes. "Now don't you worry about me. Plenty of things I can do until Mr. Slocum puts me somewhere else."

"Yeah? Give me one."

"I don't know, but there's always things to do around the house that I never have time for. I guess I could go to a few ballgames, maybe baby-sit Jenny's kids a little. Heck, Lola, maybe I can even clean this place up some. Wouldn't it be great to have the place just like it used to be, nice and tidy so we could start having friends and family over again?"

Lola's face reddened and her eyes stared blankly. Ray could see her frightened vulnerability at the thought of him cleaning up the house. She always got quiet when he got angry and threatened to throw things out.

"Honey? Wouldn't that be great?" Ray repeated.

Lola returned to the sink and turned the water back on. She lathered her hands with dish soap and began to scrub as though poison covered them.

Ray smiled for the first time all day, surprised that losing his job might actually bring some cheer in his life. "Guess I'll run out and pick up something for us," he said, conceding on the dinner front. "Was it Wendy's you said you wanted?"

When Ray stepped outside again the clouds had gone, leaving a bright, tranquil sky. Back on the road he breathed calmly and felt his hunger restored. He imagined Lola finding a job or doing some part-time babysitting while he waited to get back to work. He envisioned getting up at ten o'clock instead of seven, and dreamed about the warmth and extra space he'd have in bed if Lola got up first. He thought about a clean house, seeing the light blue, living room carpet again. He could finally walk through the house without caution, pull open the drapes without knocking things over, and find his old photo albums, books, and videos again.

After two left turns, Ray pulled into the Wendy's parking lot. Despite the dinnertime rush, he went inside rather than using the drive-thru window. In line he looked up and stared at the menu even though his order never changed.

"Thank you for choosing Wendy's. May I take your order?"

"Yes, I'd like two Singles, two regular fries, a Frosty, and a Jr. Bacon Cheeseburger to go please." The clerk repeated the order as she punched each item on the register. "Actually, no. I'm sorry," Ray interrupted. "No need for the Jr. Bacon Cheeseburger."

Ray collected the order and returned to his car. The smell of burgers and fries made him hungrier, but rush hour traffic prevented any speeding. He turned on the radio to his classic rock station and sang along to Molly Hatchet's "Flirtin' with Disaster."

Ray arrived home and walked into the house smiling. Lola was not at the sink or on the sofa. "Dinner's here," he shouted towards the bedroom.

Lola opened the bedroom door and turned sideways to get through the hallway. She took a plate from the cabinet over the sink and a can of Coke from the refrigerator. "Which ones are mine?" she asked, looking at the three Wendy's bags still in Ray's hands.

Ray handed her the two bags with her Single, fries, and Frosty, then watched as she returned to the bedroom. He had expected her dismal mood. Opening the refrigerator for his own Coke, Ray prepared to eat at the sink again. He opened the

Wendy's bag and relished the smell of greasy meat. He unwrapped the burger, took a huge bite, and grabbed a few fries. Meals at the kitchen sink would soon be a thing of the past as well. It would be no easy task, would take several weeks, but he'd get that house cleaned up before Mr. Slocum reassigned him so he could finally have a place to sit down. Ray took a second bite of his hamburger, its juices collecting in the corner of his mouth. Then the bedroom door squeaked.

"Ray Feasley, where the hell is my Jr. Bacon Cheeseburger?"

Ray stepped out of the kitchen and peered down the hall. "Lola, I figured I'd just get you the Single since we need to start cutting back a little while I'm between jobs. Unless maybe you want to do a little babysitting."

"There ain't going to be no between jobs, Ray."

"Now, Lola, I told you not to worry about that. Mr. Slocum will put me back to work in a month or two."

"No, he ain't either. Found his business card on the dresser where you try and keep your little things so cute and organized. Told him it was a disgrace after all you've done for that company. He's putting you on as a cashier at the St. Albans branch starting Monday. Now go back and get my Jr. Bacon Cheeseburger before my fries are as cold as my Frosty."

Ray bit his tongue and tasted blood. He threw his burger and fries back into the bag and walked out the door, his chin hanging down to his chest. After opening his car door, he got inside and sank down in the seat, then closed his eyes to a vision of Lola's thick arm laid firmly across him every morning like a two-by-four.

FISSURES

Yellow poplar, white ash, and northern red oak still swayed in the distance, touching the moon on flawless nights. But they stood with mostly forgotten messages, their invitations sent through scattered leaves and swollen seeds often chewed up or sold. The short distance to reach them, to get away from gossip and petty spats, had grown longer: forest cleared into fields, then lots, gravel dust, a driveway for the sheriff's car.

Jasper walked to what remained, to leave frustrations at his family's home, the last house on a dead-end street in their subdivision. He wanted no more sappy mailbox art, no more engine smoke. A stumbling fawn or patch of bright mushrooms needed instead—scenic mountainside and forest to untangle his tension. The concrete grew distant, replaced by soil and snapping twigs under his shoes. Hair blew across his forehead. Still, his mind swelled with the words of home, words that festered. He was the first in the family to go to college, not a cheating husband on Pentecostal land.

"History?" his father had shouted an hour earlier in the doorway of his bedroom. "If you're going to study that, it won't be from a penny of mine. I'll not pay good money for you to go and get some piece of paper says you studied history. What kind of job you going to get with that?"

Jasper sat on the bed motionless, head down. Over the years he had learned that playing possum was better than open conflict. Upon seeing his prey lifeless, his father might pause and fake a lighter tone, although venom still lurked under false mercy.

"Son, I just don't want you to think life is easy. Before you know it, you'll have a family too, and you'll want to take care of them best you can. You don't want to go back living in them hollers like I did. We can get in the car and I'll drive you up Mud Lick right now if I have to. Remind you what it's like. Burning coal and feeding hogs. Sit down on a ring of ice just to do your thing in wintertime. I mean ice!"

"Can't you be a minister at Lazy Bottom Methodist or a door-to-door Childcraft salesman with a history degree?" Jasper wanted to snap back, but he couldn't speak, felt a deep emptiness he couldn't solve.

"Jasper, I wish I had the opportunity and abilities you have. All kinds of things a sharp kid like you can get into. There's business, law, medicine, engineering. Your mother and me would be proud as punch. Just pick which one you like." Once he had trampled Jasper's willpower, it all sounded so simple.

Bruised and melancholic, Jasper stepped off the wider trail and onto a faint path he had worn down over the years. In six weeks it would be covered by the fiery colors of autumn leaves. A fallen sassafras tree remained strewn on the ground, rotten and invaded by carpenter ants. Jasper ripped off a small piece of its bark for a whiff of sweetness to help clear his mind, setting off a frenzy inside the insects' smooth tunnels. *A dead tree on the forest floor isn't a cemetery*, he thought. He could cut his hair and deposit it here in the undergrowth, leave a tiny chunk of flesh, even a scab, and something would be made from it.

It was a reasonable argument to explain that plenty of students studied history before law school, but even in the unlikely chance it worked, Jasper knew he couldn't play a four-year charade. He didn't know what he "wanted to be," as they conveniently put it, only the many things he didn't want.

Jasper breathed easier in the fresh air as the sun worked hard to get through the forest canopy. Dogwood, magnolia, and witch hazel dominated the understory, and he noticed that the smell of bugwort, pungent and uniquely sweet, had faded somewhat since his last visit. A breeze brought soothing birdsong through the trees, and Jasper wished he'd never hear the grating motors of lawnmowers, weed whackers, or leaf blowers again.

"Ought to get you a job with Carbide, Jasper," his grandmother kept telling him. "Just like your granddad, except engineer instead of foreman. They make good money." He knew his mother had told her to pressure him. "It's for his own good," he heard her say over the telephone.

"Get you a business degree and you can take over Dad's job in a few years, turn it into something bigger if you want," Mother told him on other occasions, apparently unaware that he'd rather wrestle crocodiles for a living than sell and market children's encyclopedias.

Jasper stuck to the path, heard a chipmunk shoot back into the rocks. Grey catbirds skulked and mewed, their beaks dancing on the soil. The trail led down the hill and forked at the creek, the left path leading to distant hills and the right to a ridge overlooking the interstate built a decade earlier. Jasper dashed across the creek and up the embankment to the right where he noticed the pointy tips of a shed antler on the ground. He walked over and cleared the soil around it, picked it up to find that squirrels and mice had whittled it in half. Thoughts merged into dreams when the bone of antlers or the black flint of arrowheads, still sharp enough to pierce the skin, lay in his hand.

Jasper hurried to reach the lookout, a favorite spot for birds enjoying the open brush on the side of the mountain. He pressed on for fifteen minutes until the trees thinned, reaching the majestic view. He climbed upon the outcrop of rocks and sat down on the emerald moss, placing his backpack beside him. Below, little mites of steel raced over the highway, reminding him of the carpenter ants that rushed over their smooth, hollowed out paths inside the fallen sassafras tree. Across the interstate the dirty river lined the base of the mountain like a crooked, tightly secured brown belt. A small aircraft sailed in through the clouds, falling behind the hill for landing.

He recalled afternoons at home with his mother when they would hear the blasts, the dynamite shaking the walls of their house as they gorged the mountains to build the highway, leaving scattered chunks and spilled entrails. Thinking of it now still brought rings of heat and memories of specters approaching the front door to solicit his parents' signatures—an agreement to scar the design of millions of years.

A male Eastern Tiger Swallowtail drifted out from below the overhang as Jasper rubbed the soft green patch next to him and readjusted his haunches. *Make it out of the hollows at what cost?* he thought. His father had not pioneered the idea of progress, this race to expand, control, even destroy the mountains, but its momentum had gained almost universal approval.

Two hours later, the sun had started its descent to the ridgeline when Jasper stood up to return home. He slowly made his way back through the forest, passed a skunk foraging for beetles: that independent, curious rover that people belittled but could not attack since it had one major card to play. He wished he could find his own single card. He thought of his mother and how she shunned the entire forest like people shun that feared animal, how the mountains meant little more to her than an occasional picnic in a park clearing. The soil itself was considered dirty, unsafe, and unsanitary, while faith could be placed in an assortment of colored pills to maintain health.

Back in the field on the edge of the subdivision, he felt a pang in his stomach that signaled his pending arrival home. A wrapper flittered in a small patch of buttercups and Jasper picked it up, the flimsy plastic still sticky with honeybun. He cut through his neighbor's backyard and then his family's, the smell of cut grass still strong. His father had mowed the lawn, growing impatient with Jasper's absence.

Jasper's legs dragged as he climbed the concrete steps to the garage. At the top of the stairs he sat down and removed his shoes. Another hour or so and the sun would rest for the night. He could smell the heat of the old Chevy in the garage, but he didn't care what little trip his father had made. When he opened the back door to the house, the smell of grease in the kitchen cut through the coolness from the air conditioner.

"Jasper, where you been?" his mother said as she put a bowl of fried potatoes on the kitchen table. "Dinner's ready."

"Not hungry, Mom."

Jasper's father sat at the table, ignoring his son's arrival as he listened to the headlines. War coverage had dominated the first fifteen minutes of the evening news for the past two weeks.

"You know you have to eat. Go and wash up," his mother directed him as usual.

Jasper passed through the kitchen quickly, then slowed on his way to the bathroom. He must delay until news of the war finished or else his dad would coax him into argument. The bathroom was his best option, an easy place to lock the door and delay with a legitimate excuse.

After several minutes he heard his mother calling again.

"Jasper! Dinner's on the table and waiting."

"Be there in a minute, Mom," Jasper yelled back, stalling.

Five minutes later he sat down at the dinner table and drank half his glass of sweet tea.

"Where you been?" his father asked, taking no time to begin the drill. Jasper didn't answer, scooping out two spoonfuls of canned peas from a bowl. A minute passed without talk while he half-filled his plate.

"I did the mowing for you. Got tired of waiting. Grass is already high. If I wait on you, there'll be snakes making out in the front lawn."

"I was out in the forest."

"Saying prayers or searching for three-dollar bills?"

"Honey, just let him eat first," Jasper's mother interceded.

"Oh, yeah, sorry about that. Mr. Dreams needs all the energy he can get to contemplate mountains."

Jasper thought to get up from the table as his father reached over with his fork to stab a second pork chop.

"Save one for Jasper, dear," his mother said.

"I don't want any, Mom."

"Oh, Jasper, get you a pork chop." Her hair fell down into her eyes, and without makeup the lines on her face stood out.

Jasper put a bite of yellow tomato into his mouth with little appetite. Eating simply to prevent further hostility had grown commonplace. He kept his head bowed and chewed methodically, his eyes a few inches from the plate and the fork just under his nose. His plan as always: eat little and finish quickly, escape to his room.

"Jasper, you got some more mail from the school today," his mother finally said. "I didn't open it, but maybe it's about them scholarships you applied for."

Jasper knew it could only be more glossy advertising trash coming from the college where he recently paid his enrollment deposit.

"Light them up!" his father called out to news of renewed air assaults on Iraqi Republican Guard positions outside Baghdad.

Jasper didn't hear his father. Instead, he sat thinking that he should forget college, pull his enrollment, get a cheap-paying job, and move out. It would confuse them at first, then hurt his mother deeply. Jasper's eyes moistened, but he didn't want to break down in front of his father. Head down, he couldn't see the faces of his parents, but out of the corner of his eye his father's hands moved

43

to butter another piece of white bread, the fingers crawling around the table like pale spider legs. Again, Jasper remembered the ants under the bark of the sassafras tree, thought how his father's fingers moved in the same way, thought of the damage men do.

Jasper swallowed his last bite of food, forgetting what he had placed in his mouth. Skin on his face tightening, he had lost the will to stand up from the table. Behind him the back door opened and the mountains surged inside, rushing to fill the hollow space inside his chest, a place cut and beat up too.

Upstairs

Pale but for protruding blue veins, a wrinkled, bony hand slowly lifted the last bite of lemon cake. Charlie had brought it early yesterday afternoon for her, and she wanted to eat it while it was still fresh, unaware of yesterday's expiration date marked on the package. The empty wrapper and its ninety-nine-cent sticker lay on the kitchen table beside her eyeglasses and a key. Thursday's newspaper was off to the side, opened to a partially completed crossword puzzle.

She chewed and swallowed the cake without expression— Charlie preoccupied her mind. He had left thirty minutes ago, staying less than twenty-four hours, for more rain was coming, he said. She thought of the time that would pass before he returned, the months blurring together in her mind. Her head turned slowly as she looked across the table, then out the window at the muddy hill behind the house. The sun shone through a clouded grey, a vague mess for eyes that could make out only shapes and colors.

She slid her palm across the smoothness of the table to find her glasses. Both hands gripped the arms of her chair as she stood up groaning. Picking up the plastic wrapper she carefully flattened it out on the table, then crumpled it into a ball and carried it to the garbage can in the corner of the kitchen. After sliding open the container's lid she thought better than to throw away the last remnant of her son's visit and returned it to the table. She wondered if her caretaker would stop in today, wondered what she'd say about this piece of plastic in the center of an orderly, ascetic room.

She picked up the key from the table. It was a vintage brass key that opened Charlie's old bedroom, long enough to match the old lock of an old house. Since moving out twenty years ago,

Charlie insisted the room remain locked and untouched. When he stayed the night he would even change the bed sheets himself. She complied with her son's requests, but on occasion, for sentimental reasons, she climbed the wooden stairs to his room, unlocked the door, and entered.

Over the years she'd grown emotional about the changes Charlie made to the room, an accumulation of little adaptations. The queen-sized bed was now against the wall, a calendar and clock replaced the music and movie posters, papers and old business journals covered the small desk, and two filing cabinets stood in the corner.

With the key in the palm of her swollen right hand, she left the kitchen. She turned the dining room corner, arrived at the stairs, and grabbed onto the railing. Slowly she began to climb. On the first step she told herself she wouldn't linger for long in his room, for Charlie's sake. On the second step she reminded herself that her son was good; he was educated and successful, and the proof was in his new car that took him far away. On the third step she thought how his father would be proud of him. She steadied herself with the help of the railing, ready to ascend the fourth stair, until sunlight engulfed her arched body: the front door opened behind her and Charlie's bearded face left her hazy mind.

"Charlie gone?" The words shot at her like a spear.

"Yeah."

"Now Iris, what are you doing on them stairs? I've told you a million times not to climb by yourself. There's nothing up there you need that's worth breaking a hip for. Tell me what you want and I'll run up and get it."

She didn't like the cackling voice of that overweight bossiness. She felt sheepish—reprimanded like a child in the house where she once commanded a husband and three sons. She turned around, not to respond, but to retreat, wanting to hide or get away.

"Tell me what it is and I'll go get it."

The door closed and a light flicked on.

"You don't have to live like a bat in a cave, Iris. Turn them lights on sometimes."

"Just like to go up every once in a while," she said, her voice faint as she felt a tug on her wrist.

"I see you got that key in your hand. You going up to Charlie's room now, aren't you?"

Iris remembered the wrapper on the table.

"Don't you worry about him. He's a big boy now."

"I know it."

"You want me to take you up there now, Iris? Nothing new up there."

"No. That's Charlie's room," she said, reaching the bottom stair.

"That's right. You're right. That's Charlie's room."

She stopped and scratched her arm, then looked up at the photos hanging on the wall. She didn't want to be followed to the kitchen.

"Now where you want me to put that key, Iris?"

"That's all right. Put it away myself."

"Okay, well, you need anything else? I'm on my way to Kroger's and wanted to see if you need anything before next Tuesday."

"Thank ya."

"So anything you want me to get you?"

"Some more peaches I reckon."

"Them canned ones?"

"Yeah."

"Anything else?"

"No."

"Well, all right. Say, you got a rash or anything on your arm, Iris?"

"No."

"Well, you're gonna make one if you keep scratching it like that. I'll take a look at it Tuesday to see if there's anything wrong. Now you go on in the kitchen and sit down."

"I'm going."

"Charlie brought up your mail and paper I see."

"Yeah. He's a good boy."

"Yes, he is. Okay, I'll be back in an hour or so with them peaches. Don't you go up them stairs while I'm gone. Charlie'll come visit you again later."

"When's he coming?"

"Well, now, I don't know. We'll have to ask Charlie."

She took a step towards the kitchen and put the key in her pocket, thinking about the wrapper on the table again. She'd have to hide it before fatty came back with the peaches. She heard the door close as she walked past her porcelain collection that never got used anymore.

There was the wrapper. She sat down at the table and stared at it. When she removed her glasses, the wrapper was a silver fish. Instead of gutting it she folded it up into a tiny square. Then she placed it inside her pocket next to the key and a piece of butterscotch candy.

She stared out the window again and her mind drifted. She saw her husband crossing Quarrier Street, then picking cucumbers in the garden. Someone changed a diaper in the church vestibule, a typewriter sat on the desk in an empty office, and a middle-aged woman swallowed brightly colored pills. The air in the room felt dry on her skin. Rays of sunlight hit her eyes, and she gripped the chair beneath her as if to test its firmness.

She did not hear the knock on the door, only the subsequent holler.

"You in the kitchen, Iris?"

Before she could answer or turn around, a thump landed on the counter and the woman hovered at her side.

"Boy, them canned peaches were two for a dollar, can you believe that? You must've known they were having a sale, Iris. I got you ten cans."

She noticed the woman looking at the table and thought about the wrapper in her pocket. Her hand went inside to make sure it hadn't gotten away.

"Well, my word. I left that puzzle on the table and didn't even finish it on Thursday. Have to finish it Tuesday I reckon. You want me to open one of them cans of peaches now, Iris? Ain't any in the frig is there?"

She saw the door swing open and felt a chill as the woman stuck her head inside the refrigerator.

"Got some cooked apples in here, but no peaches. Let me take the rest of them downstairs and then I'll open a can up for you."

The door to the basement opened and more cool air wafted into the kitchen. She heard the fragile stairs creak even more than usual due to the excess weight. Her mind strained to follow the woman downstairs, then it stalled and she forgot her.

"I'm getting old, Iris," the woman said after returning moments later, breathing heavy. "Let me open them peaches."

Her eyes grew large, surprised by the woman's appearance from the bowels of her home. Uneasy, she strained to recognize her.

"Hope Charlie comes back soon, don't you, Iris? I almost didn't recognize him with that sharp haircut of his."

"Yeah."

"Here's you a bowl of peaches now. Just a minute and I'll get you some cottage cheese to go with them."

"Thank ya."

The woman placed the leftover peaches inside the refrigerator and took out a plastic container of cottage cheese. Three large spoonfuls of the white lumps went inside a bowl and then onto the table beside the peaches.

"Now I'll be back on Tuesday like always, but you give me a call if you need anything, dear. Okay?"

"Okay," she answered, looking at the cottage cheese and peaches. She put her glasses on again, picked up the spoon, and cut a peach wedge into fourths before dipping a piece into the cottage cheese. The woman stared at her, making her hesitant to eat. "Thank ya."

"Oh, you're welcome, Iris. Now let me get going. Jenny'll be over before I know it, and I gotta get supper on down home too. I'll see you Tuesday."

"Okay."

"You call me if you need anything now."

"When's Charlie coming back?"

"Well, now, I don't guess anyone knows but Charlie. He'll be back to see you though, don't you worry. Bye-bye, Iris."

"Okay."

"Be good. See you Tuesday."

"Okay."

She put her spoon down and removed her glasses, searching for a certain memory, hoping for her son's return. When the kitchen clock struck the hour ten minutes later, she noticed the peaches and cottage cheese still in front of her. She ate them slowly, then carried the two empty bowls to the sink and rinsed them off. She looked around at the walls of the kitchen, searching for a photograph. It was time to climb the stairs again—Charlie was home.

She made it to the top of the stairs despite the pain in her left hip. A mirror would have shown her the changes that time had brought to her body: the wrinkles on her face, particularly the ones around her eyes, the sunken cheeks, and the hunched shoulders which seemed to grow a life of their own. But without the mirror, she saw another time.

"Charlie?" she called, anticipating an adolescent's voice.

There was much to discuss if she could get him to answer behind the door. So he did, and she followed the voice, needing to talk. Her gnarled hand came up from her side and placed the key in the keyhole. With a twist of her wrist she unlocked the door. It felt both heavy and light as she pushed it open to a large room darkened by closed curtains. Little Charlie had made his bed.

Her eyes looked behind the door to the desk covered with disorganized papers: letters from lawyers, changes in her will, documents of stock and life insurance policies, and receipts for cemetery plot transactions. She hadn't considered such matters for over two years, had grown incapable of following the drivel, but she felt a force that jumped from the desk, wanting to escape through the opened door. She took two steps inside the room to meet it as her eyes locked on the photographs hanging on the far wall. She heard a television, then a commercial selling cooking knives. A faint voice told her not to buy.

Through her cataracts and failing vision she saw the shadows in front of the window—Charlie's skinny hand on a smooth chin. His hair was parted neatly on the side, just as she had combed it, and his face turned from middle-aged to young adult to adolescent. Obsession, love, and instinct all helped make him real.

She turned to look at the bed in the corner again. Her husband lay atop the flannel sheets. It was time to continue their conversations while Charlie played nearby. Her back ached and the throbbing in her right leg doubled as she climbed into the bed to lie down next to him. With Charlie babbling over his toy trucks, Iris took her side of the bed for the last time.

The caretaker would find the upstairs door open on Tuesday, find her body stiff, her frail vision vanished. Memories of advertisements and Charlie would float through the room amidst stacks of old papers, the only things that seemed to live forever.

Charles would take the phone call on a busy morning in his office. And after his coffee he would make preparations for the next day to drive to his mother's home, much clean up to do.

DAYBREAK

Every morning, even before the birds start whining, we hear the long coal trains rambling over nearby tracks. And on Mondays the sanitation truck follows, stopping and starting its engine as it circles our subdivision. Well, I'm not sure what Linda hears—she's always dead asleep, pills or no pills. The neighbors' dogs bark for the twenty minutes it takes the garbage crew to make its rounds, plus five more after they've gone—all while I lie here in the darkness surrounded by gazebo prints and kitty drawings, dolls Linda inherited from her grandmother, and photos of the children from some other man on vacations I wasn't around for. I try to rest up for another hour or two, but always end up thinking about things until it's time to go downstairs and brew the morning coffee.

Yeah, sure, the bedroom is the woman's domain, my own father tried to tell me that years ago. "That's just the way it's always been," he said. "The bedroom ain't for nothing but sleep and that other stuff anyway, so just put you a TV and frig with cold beer in the basement and forget about it."

"Other stuff?" I don't even know what that is any more. You'd think we're thirty years into the marriage, but it's only been four. Jerry Glass says he's got the same problem and that we might as well think about it like we do the Big Red Machine—you know, hall of fame and nostalgia. Johnny Bench, I suppose.

Linda rolls over and toots her horn. I guess Jerry would just chalk it up to a seventh-inning stretch. She's been doing that a lot more lately since they put her on that new medicine—almost as frequently as she reminds everyone that her name means "beautiful" in Spanish. "Yeah, and my name means 'shut the hell up' in Cherokee," I tell her, which results in one more "Oh, Ronald."

51

Just about the time the howling of the train and truck stops is when the morning light starts to seep into the bedroom. I feel it coming every morning, like a biting dog. Our second-floor bedroom looks out over the eastern horizon, perfect for sun torture. I told Linda a long time ago to put up some dark curtains to keep the light out, simple as that, but no, she says she likes those airy, see-through, sheen ones that are "sexy and give off great atmosphere."

She sure doesn't mind piling on either: "Ron, you're just a light sleeper like Betty Campbell. She started wearing those sleep goggles and her problem went away. She says you should give them a try."

Good to know Betty Campbell can relate to me. She's the Mary Kay agent who's convinced I always drive off the road onto her grass. She's been trying to convince Linda to wear these nighttime facial masks to stop the aging process since before almost any war you can think of.

"I can't believe you used to dream of being an airline pilot when you were a boy," Linda says. "How would you ever fly a plane if the sun annoys you so much?"

"Because they're not trying to sleep when they're piloting!" I yell, but it's like reasoning with a lawn inspector: easy answers even for chinch bugs and crab grass. And that's after they act like you've caused them to appear yourself. I guess if Linda worked at the care home with me, God forbid, she'd have answers for dementia, diarrhea, blindness, and foot odor as well. And she'd tell us all how to clean ass without so much as wetting a cloth.

Of course, I've thought about moving out of the bedroom and sleeping on the sofa in the living room, but it's one of those shorties we got at K-Mart and I can't sleep with my legs hanging out into the air. Well, truth told, I've thought about divorcing and moving out altogether. But I'm sure everyone can understand the economics behind it—half the house payment, utilities, all of it would go right out that door with her. Somehow you've got to pay for all of life's conveniences—and the coal trains and garbage trucks. Just like someone named Ronald has to whip up the eggs and milk to make pancakes of a morning, then empty bedpans at night. In between all that is just a bunch of small talk and medicine, drugs, whatever you want to call them.

"At least you know what you've got to look forward to," Gil Kresper says to me while I'm clipping his toenails. He's been in room 118 for over a year now. He's fought off gangrene, bedsores, prostate cancer, cataracts, you name it, but can't recall that we've had the same shitty conversation almost every day since he's arrived.

"I'm never going down that road," I always tell Jerry. He commutes to the care home from Keyser, but he's always in a good mood nonetheless. "I'll call it quits first. You'll find something alive in Gil's bedpan before you see me in that condition."

Jerry'll smirk, Mountain Dew in hand. "There's all kinds of stuff living in Gil's bedpan, Ronnie."

"Yeah, yeah, under his toenails then. You know what I mean."

"Nah. That's what I used to think too. But when the day comes, you'll do whatever it takes to get to tomorrow. Just take Gil's advice: if you haven't got you a good woman, go out and find you one while there's still time."

I never mentioned Linda to him. I don't wear a ring and haven't told anybody at work about my four-year-old disaster. Just don't want to talk about it. But every time the topic comes up I think about Karen, the sweet one from high school. Then I can't help but think of Missy, my first mistake who was basically just a younger version of this second mistake. But sad to say, as sure as that sun's playing devil in my eyes now, I don't know how in the hell I'd get anything better even if I could start getting a decent night's sleep. Fifty has come and gone, my slipped disks have taken on a life of their own, and I work at a goddamn old-age home.

I never used to think about any of this stuff. It's only after lying half-awake in this bedroom every morning for the last four years, listening to the engines and the dogs, that the mind starts to get the better of you. Well, maybe the job has something to do with it too. You know—people dying, people sick; people sick of dying and dying of sick.

Everyone sees I've got a problem: red eyes with bags under them, colds almost every month, frequent fever blisters. People ask me if I've got a drinking problem, and I've given serious thought to starting one just so I could give them a simple answer. Other than Jerry, I don't discuss it with anyone. Certainly not Linda. That's not saying much though because I just tell Jerry I've got insomnia, which is not the real story. He's drunk half the time anyway and his hands usually smell like shit because he doesn't wash them much at work, so I don't want to get him all excited. When he's excited he talks a lot with his hands, waves them around and all.

I also gave serious thought to attending church—the Presbyterian one on the corner of 4th Street since they're not the type that goes door-to-door or hands out those damn pamphlets all over the place. I thought if I go there I might be able to unload this stuff off my chest. You know, they listen to all kinds of sob stories. That's what church is for. As a matter of fact, I got myself all dressed up one Sunday morning about three months ago, drove into town, parked the car and everything. But then on the short walk to the church I ran into Cassie Smalls who works in the offices at the care home. No need to embarrass anyone by describing her, but let me just say, she's the only woman on earth to have that special kind of interest in me, and the last thing I need is to sit in a damn pew looking for solace while some googly-eyed accountant follows me into church to stare at me with lustful vision.

"You're looking sharp this morning, Ronnie. Smell darn good, too. Old Spice?"

"Yeah, I'm walking down to the post office," I said, knowing she'd be asking soon enough.

"Post office? The post office isn't even open on Sunday."

"Yeah, I know. I meant Walmart."

"Walmart? Ronnie, I think I've got you flustered."

"Yeah, I fluster pretty easy of a morning."

My only child, Cindy, from my previous marriage with Missy, lives in South Carolina, and even though I only talk to her once or twice a year, I thought of her just then. She's a tarot card reader and believes in all those goofy signs and what-not, and at that moment I realized that running into Cassie meant church probably wasn't for me.

I'm replaying the whole story again, can even see Cassie's over-sized, flowery blouse, when the stone beside me rolls away and Linda rises up from the bed. She does it without an alarm clock somehow, and I'm not allowed to set mine any earlier than when she gets up; I wouldn't anyway. She does her little morning stretches, impressive if she were dead or bed-ridden, and lets off some more gas as she rotates her hip area, hands over head like she thinks it's somehow civilized.

When she leaves five minutes later for the first of her three morning trips to the bathroom, I scoot a bit to the center of the bed to feel the warmth she's left.

"I wish you'd flush when you go to the bathroom during the night," she says, returning to the bedroom fifteen minutes later. That's my cue to finally get up. "You know I've got enough on my mind without having to smell your overnight stories."

"I didn't even go to the bathroom during the night, Linda."

"Must have been before you came to bed then."

"I don't know what you're talking about."

"Just flush it, Ronald. All right? Not that hard."

I'm sitting on the side of the bed in my striped boxers, rubbing my eyes with the palm of my hand.

"And hurry up and brew the coffee."

I think again of the coal trains that shoot by each morning. I imagine them filled with coffee beans. Then I imagine garbage bags filled with coffee grinds and paper filters, the trucks carrying our trash off Monday morning to some lonely, unknown place in the earth that might as well be the resting place for my own tired body.

Or maybe Linda's.

Relocation

I didn't mind much Mother's weekend palm readings in Shepherdstown—it was her talking to plants that always embarrassed me. "Well, hello! You're enjoying this beautiful sunny day, aren't you?" The sticky-sweet chat to her peace lilies is still saccharine-stuck in my mind.

"Just find one, Amy. Just one. One man worth appreciating," she would say. "One that rests comfortably in your hand, stretches all the way across it, from one end of life to the other." Then she'd hold out her palm to demonstrate, walk two fingers across it like I was six years old instead of twenty-four.

I see her now as I turn the lock and push open the door to an empty apartment. I see the City Paper folded neatly under her arm so the sex-call ads peep out, a stranger's hot nipple nibbling at her elbow from the backend pages of a city.

It's the cheapest apartment I could find in Keyser on such quick notice. I hear her say, "Why would anyone waste money on renting?"

I hear Gordon, too, her third husband, and see him in his blue blazer. "Would you rent a child? How about a bed? Your dog? No? Then why would you rent your home?"

I turn on the living room light. I don't remember the brown carpet and its browner splotches from yesterday. Or the door to the cabinet under the kitchen sink removed and propped up against the wall, the scrambling silverfish and confident cockroaches and pill bugs, the damp, the dump. I just didn't notice.

But I'm in, so I'm out. Mike can go to hell with his hopeless self-help seminars.

I roll up the torn blinds in the living room for a view—a slumbering cemetery, its tombstones the little discolored teeth of a corpse. There are worse things. Does the mood of a grave depend on the angle of light? Each morning when I go out to the car I'll reach over the short fence to rub my palm over the dry chunks of granite, run my finger tips through crevices that spell out the names of Harper, Lee, and Sanford. So what? Right now the idea makes me crave a strawberry.

The cable technician pulls up five minutes after me, right at the outset of his four-hour appointment window. Through the screen door I watch the young man gathering tools from his vehicle. Under a crooked cap his eyes are bright. His mouth is set in a subtle smile that tells me he's the talkative type. I let him in anyway.

With the usual muddy boots and name-tagged shirt, he takes a look at the wiring and says things should be straightforward.

"Right?"

"Sure."

"Just moving in here?"

"Yeah."

"First month is free, you know. Trial run for you new subscribers."

"I know."

"We haven't serviced this place in five years. Who's been living here?"

"Don't know anything about that," I answer. I just know I might need those television voices to keep me company over the next thirty days.

"You don't mind living next to the cemetery?"

"No, I don't. It doesn't bite."

"Well, it might."

"Anything might."

"This place better than where you were before?"

"Yeah. Better than bedbugs."

The man with the name of Ken patched on his shirt stops clicking his staple gun and looks up. I wonder what dirt is floating around in his inquisitive, brown eyes.

"At your old place?"

"Yeah."

He looks more closely at my bare arms. Hematophagous scabs, he probably thinks. Kind of right. "Worse than chiggers I hear," he says.

"Yeah."

But *cimex lectularius* isn't the real reason I moved. Unless you consider *him* a bedbug. That works. Yeah, the "sucking your blood" connection is easy. But there's also the crawling on you in the middle of the night for nothing more than a lascivious meal and then hiding in tiny crevices where he can't be seen the rest of the day. Then the scratching—they work mostly on appendages, but for *him* I have to scratch my head or between my legs. And it's impossible to get rid of either of them. You have to move out, and still there's no guarantee they won't follow.

"I guess once your family gets moved in, things won't be so bad. Get your furniture and a few plants in here. Pets if you got any."

I don't answer. I turn my head and look through the window at the cemetery instead, ignoring whatever else he's got to say.

My cell phone beeps. It's Mom. I wait a minute, then listen to her message.

"I haven't heard from you in a week," she begins.

I cut it short, stash the phone back in my pocket, and walk closer to the window to look outside again at the death markers lined up like dominoes. People pay a lot to be put there. Pay more than just money.

"All done. You're all set," he says ten minutes later, turning on the television to make sure it functions. Something holds his gaze longer. "Ah, it's *Bounce*. Good flick. Seen it?"

"Nah."

I think how I'll lay a blanket down in a few hours on the spot where he is kneeling. But for now, once he's gone, I think I'll stare some more out the window. Maybe a tick-less doe will wind up its legs and skip across the grass-covered skeletons. Sure, gone in a moment. But not. Me climbing on its back.

I don't mind the cemetery. The little tombs are polished rocks chiseled from mighty mountains of another place and time, and the tiny letters scribbled on them mean nothing to me.

TUNNEL

I'm asleep when we pull in early Monday morning. The arrival announcement wakes me, and I lift my craned neck from against the clouded window. I've returned again, like it or not. The seat next to me is still empty and the bus' heater has left me basting in my own sweat. Outside I see the glass to the upgraded Greyhound station, foggy from a late winter's dawn. A few people stand on the corner waiting for local buses, maybe one or two of them headed to work.

I'm not so old that I can't grab my bag quickly when the bus comes to a stop, shoot for some air that's less stale, but I'm stuck in the aisle for five minutes waiting for the woman with three kids to pull her bags down from overhead. When I finally get off, I'm met by the smells of instant coffee, cigarettes, and an old Steelers jacket over the crisp cold. No one looks or says a thing to me as I collect my Converse bag from under the bus and move on.

Throat dry, I walk back up Main Street looking over my shoulder at the new Wesco Arena built along the river. The water of the Ohio is up to its rim. Across the street Staab's Chiropractor still stands dark and abandoned, its doorway decorated with cobwebs and sawdust. On the next block, Music Hall has kept its tacky photos of Elvis impersonators from odd Tuesdays pasted to its windows. Funny what sets a person to contemplation, but I begin to remember my hometown in flashes, this place that was just hunting ground before that first bridge was built over the Ohio. Then the wagons started coming, the taverns were put up, and people went mad digging for fossil fuels. These are still hunting grounds, but we all have forgotten what it is we're hunting for now and why the phantoms keep floating through with cold blood.

This town isn't rock bottom though. It's not Welch, or Elizabeth, or Williamson. Aside from the river that floats on and around, people still pass through here a bit more than a little. Maybe they don't stick around much, but at least there's circulation to keep the blood moving. Pittsburgh's only an hour away and a few would argue it's this town's beating heart. Others think of it as big brother. Old money is still around a bit, and so are some Victorian houses. Someone even puts out a magazine that smells like the glossy attitude of Manhattan. I didn't consider looking for greener pastures elsewhere a big deal, but every time I come back there's a pain in more than my throat.

I come upon the historic suspension bridge and see the hotel is still on the corner, now painted a cheap lime green that doesn't sit right against the overcast sky. Like any old hotel, it's got walls and rails and could pass as a penitentiary. I'll stay here a week if need be, assuming rates are still favorable. No reason why they'd change—maybe they've even lowered. I cross the parking lot, tread through the old mulch put down for some sprouting plants, and reach the entrance. The door is heavy as I pry it open and enter.

"Check-in ain't until three, sugar," I hear a voice say behind the counter.

I step up, check her nametag before speaking. "I just got in town off the overnight bus, Robin. I could use a shower before heading over to the tracks."

"I see," she says. "Try back at noon and see if something's ready."

"Can I leave my bag with you until then?"

"Yeah, just come around and set it back here. And be back by noon to get it because my shift ends and I don't want you reporting me for no lost bag."

"Thanks, hon." I move past the vase of artificial flowers at the end of the counter, step around and bend over to set my bag on the ground. "This okay?" I say, eyeing her flip-flops. "I'll be back by eleven thirty at the latest."

I pay for the night's lodging and ask to use the restroom. It smells of overnight urine since the toilet isn't flushing too well. I add my liquid to the mixture and push down on the lever, but I'm not waiting to see how things go down. Outside, a light drizzle has started off and on, and now I realize the dampness in the air is a bone chiller.

I walk up an extra block and turn down Market Street, enter the first breakfast diner I find, Brenda's Café is wedged between two forlorn nightclubs. With no customers, I get my pick of the three booths or counter space. Bacon and eggs, toast, and three cups of black coffee will wake me up and put me to feeling heavy again. I eat quickly because that's what I'm used to doing. I don't really like the food, but somehow enjoy it. I pay the bill and leave a big two-dollar tip—it might be all Rose sees this morning. The bell on the door rings as I exit and the cold hits me again.

The old buildings on the block from 1894, 1910, and 1882 are majestic. They can't be made like that in this country anymore, yet no one wants them. Koontz Family Pharmacy is still in business on the ground floor of one. An old man works the counter, hunched over and weasel-like, filling a prescription as I pass by; still a business for that.

Walking south I pass a few more eateries, most closed, a jewelry store, and a tobacco shop holding on. The parking garage further down on the corner is full. After a couple more blocks, I come to the train station that stopped taking passengers about forty years ago, recently sold to an insurance company. Standing by the inland creek, the outside looks as grand as ever, its brass dormers and Tudor arches confident and oblivious to the frailty of their own survival.

Crossing the creek, I come to the hospital complex, busy and more populated than any other part of town. It's because we're living longer, I'm often told. I take a left and go two more blocks to reach the house—its blue paint is peeling and the porch is filled with junk and three rocking chairs, just as I remember. I climb the steps slowly and look at the door to recall all the times I ran through it to get outside. When I break my stare, I still don't feel ready to knock. Turning away, I take a few steps and sit down in one of the rocking chairs. Sturdy, consistent, and pacifying, it relaxes a stressful day or speeds up slow ones.

I lose track of time until Sis pulls back the curtain and stares out the screen door. She's stretching her neck trying to get a good look at me. I sit up in the chair so she can me see clearly, but she struggles to recognize. When she unlatches and opens the door, there's still no smile on her face. She's wearing a plaid shirt and faded jeans I've seen before. Her hair is still long and stringy, lips chapped.

"Where you been? Daddy's dying."

"I got here as quick as I could," I say, standing up to greet her.

"Excuse me? No, you mean you left out of here as quick as you could."

"Sis…"

"Hospital sent him back home Friday, said there's nothing they can do for him. He could go any day now. You're lucky you even made it in time to see him above ground again."

I look down at my shoes and sigh, find a remnant of bacon in my teeth to suck on.

"Where's the wife anyway?"

"Don't have a wife anymore, Sis, and you know it."

"Run her off I suppose. She got the kid, too?"

"You weren't there, Sis, how do you know?"

"Don't know much because you're off doing your own thing. The kid look like you?"

"I don't know. Hey, I just came to see Pops."

"Go on and see him then. He's in the bedroom. Might recognize you, might not."

If it's an invitation, her straight face isn't offering any hospitality, and she barely moves enough to let me through the doorway. When I do get in I take off my shoes and sink my feet into the old plush carpet, then head to Dad's room with Sis right behind me like a cop in heat. There's a smell to the house, a mustiness I've outgrown. I get to the door and remember what Pops said after his first heart attack.

"It don't matter about me leaving this world, son, but when you leave yourself, you best be saved."

"No need to knock," Sis says as I hesitate before pushing through into the bedroom. "Look here, Daddy! Look who's finally here to see you!"

I hate her for putting it that way, but walk up to Dad from behind as he's lying on his side. I peer over, see his eye of coal trying to steer itself upwards to look for something.

"Here now, Daddy, let's get you up now, your boy's here," Sis continues, flicking on a small, dim lamp that yellows her skin.

His body gives no resistance as we turn him and sit him up against the headboard. I sit myself down at the foot of the bed.

"There you go. Don't look half bad, does he?" Sis asks after he's up, but I'm not sure if she's talking to me or to Pops.

The old man is vaguely looking at me, but he can't speak. Maybe he recognizes me, maybe he doesn't. Like Sis said.

"Sis, I don't want to do anything to make him uncomfortable. Maybe we should let him rest."

"Awful considerate of you at the last hour," she says, but I just look back at Dad, try to turn her off.

I stand up and put my hand on his shoulder, ask him how he's feeling, make myself feel stupid. I put my hand in his and feel something of a grip come back to me as he tilts his neck my way. He doesn't want to let go, and his breathing gets a little heavier. I greet him, give him the best spirit I can. Sis is on the other side of the bed and pets his head.

"Gonna have to give you a haircut next week, Daddy. Hair's getting long."

I try to smile like she does, but I'm not as good at it, never was.

"Why don't you read him a Bible passage?" Sis asks, a fine line between suggestion and demand. "Or are you some other religion now?"

I wonder why it's so easy for some people to muddy things, but I tell myself to focus on Pops. I know he'd like me to read a selection. Sis hands me a Bible, one I recognize from childhood— might even have been mine.

"What's your suggestion?" I ask, mostly to save me the burden of selecting the passage.

"Guess you don't remember what he likes," she snaps.

I open up to Psalms, pick a random verse and start reading, trying to distance myself from processing its meaning. Psalm 56: "Be merciful unto me, O God: for man would swallow me up; he fighting daily oppresseth me."

When I finish the verse, Dad loosens his grip on my hand and I close the book. Of the three of us, I figure the words must affect me the most. I look over at the window in need of seeing something outside, something alive and moving, but the curtains are closed and spread their crimson reflection over the room.

"That it?" Sis asks.

The weight in my head is getting heavier, like a tumor is growing. "Daddy, I'll come back later today and read you some more." I'm speaking to Sis, of course; one of her tactics.

"Leaving us already?"

"Sis, I just gotta get a few things done, so I'll be back later today."

"Few things done? What do you need to do here? You're a stranger as far as this town's concerned. And anyway, where's your bags?"

"I'm staying over at an old friend's house, don't want to be in your way. You already got a lot with taking care of Dad."

"No you're not. You're staying at that hotel. You want me to call right now and prove you're lying? Been gone four years and I guess the beds in this house aren't good enough for you no more."

I don't say anything, keep walking slowly to the door. Some day I'll learn how to keep these things from bothering me, boiling me.

"Just remember dinner's at six like it always was. I'll tell everyone you're here."

"All right, Sis. Thanks."

"And don't go over to the island and gamble away what little you brought."

I close the front door carefully, then turn back towards her, but through the glass it's only her lips that move. I'd like to sit on the rocking chair some more, but I creep down the stairs instead. The wind has picked up and the rain is steadier. I hear the door open again behind me.

"Don't you have an umbrella or something?" Sis shouts, more loaded with disapproval than concern.

"I'll be all right, Sis. Don't worry, I'll make sure I'm dry for dinnertime."

I look down at my watch, half past ten—an hour to kill. I tuck my hands into my jacket and start off towards the hospital again. Between death and disability, I stroll down to the riverside to watch the water a bit, look for some innocence somewhere.

There's a dollar store on my way, so I go in to pick up a packet of disposable razors and some cinnamon candy.

"Three dollars eighty-four cents, please," Mary says.

From my front pocket I pull out four dollars, two more than I expected to pay, and drop them on the counter. "Thought everything in here was a dollar? That's what the sign says."

The double-chinned, middle-aged woman smiles. She's not handicapped, best I can estimate. "You got two items, sir, and they cost three dollars and eighty-four cents."

I take the coins she puts in my hand and slip them into my pocket. I grab the plastic bag without looking at her and turn to the door. The rain has stopped, and I walk down as close as possible to the river, sit on the bank with no one around and pop a piece of hard candy in my mouth. It's a beauty, like all rivers. Dad would like to sit here, too. Swirling and passing—a current on a mission that stops for nothing. People can get on if they want, but it doesn't give a damn either way. I should have brought one of the rocking chairs down here, just rock the rest of the day to see what it brings.

There's a barge in the distance, coming upriver, and I tell myself I'll sit and watch until it passes by. I look across at the island, the new racetracks and gambling center standing among decrepit houses and a football field. Spring hasn't bloomed, so there's not much color. The old bridge straddling the Ohio looks like it could tumble any day now, but a few cars cross it, ant-like in the distance. Behind me, mountains loom over the town. I still feel something grabbing me on the inside, a pride for this land if nothing else.

It's not long until the barge drifts near. It's long and sleek, but shows its age. It's got a body full of coal that glitters if the sun gets through the clouds and hits it just right. I know it will be ending its journey soon. It will pass through the dam another eight miles up, then fifteen more miles to unload its cargo at Dad's steel plant. I start to think again about Pops, but then tell myself not to get stuck: there's nothing more between us now, never was much actually. I get up slowly. If I didn't know better, I'd believe things here hadn't changed for thousands of years, and that they'd last another thousand.

I walk back to the hotel to arrive before my noon ultimatum. Robin sends me a coffee-breath smile across the counter. She hands me my bag and checks me in early, taking credit for the smooth operations. "I got you a room with a balcony too," she says. "You can play your guitar and sing to the stars all night."

I lather her with compliments, then walk outside to crawl up three flights of stairs, key in hand. I get inside the room without much fuss, open up the window to combat the mildew, and place the key on the table. The furniture and decor still play the 1950s. I turn on the television out of habit and fiddle with it a few minutes until I find a music channel with tunes from the 70s and 80s. Dr. Hook's "Sexy Eyes" comes on as I walk over and open the patio door to the balcony. Starting with my belt, I remove my clothes as the river rolls on.

When the song finishes, I take a towel from the bed and go to the bathroom. The garbage can next to the sink hasn't been emptied and a dead cockroach and spider are camped in the corner behind the toilet, but I'll take it just to get in the room early. I hang the towel over the shower rod and turn on the water, taking a piss to give it a minute to find lukewarm. I get inside the shower and move under the water, hoping it'll wash off the bus, my sleep, and whatever else it can manage. The soap is sticky and smells like ammonia, but I run it over my body and hair, only anxious then to rinse it off. Five minutes in the shower and I turn off the water, dry myself, and put on some new shorts. Back in the main room I turn down Blondie's "Heart of Glass" and turn back the bed sheets.

When I wake up, it's past five. Gingerly I get out of bed, turn the television's music back up, and then sit back down on the bed while my head clears. I haven't drunk a thing, but it feels like a hangover and I feel the pressure of having to be somewhere I'd rather not go. After several minutes, unimpressed with the song selection, I drag myself to the bathroom and water my face to see if something will grow. The mirror is chipped and stained, and I'm glad I can't study myself. I brush my teeth, comb my hair, and put on clean clothes before turning the television off and grabbing the key.

Outside, the cold forces my appetite to speak up again. Di Carlos' Pizza, Chinese, or Mexican would be my choices, but I've got a reserved seat at my childhood table without legal representation. I walk slowly despite knowing I don't want to be late, and stop into a Go-Mart to pick out a couple bags of chocolate chip cookies for the kids and an iced tea for myself. Sugar and caffeine are old friends that carry me better than anyone.

The front door is open when I arrive, and young ones are peeking out. They yell and dance when they see me turn up the sidewalk, and I regret this trip even more. Quickly their shadows flitter away and Sis' husband Jack comes to the door.

"Come on in, Rob. She's putting dinner on the table now."

"Thanks, Jack, how you been?" I ask as I step inside, a couple of the kids hanging around the corner.

"We're doing okay here, can't complain. How's life in the big city?"

"To be honest, I couldn't tell you. Hard to figure it out."

"How come you're staying there then?" he asks with curiosity, noticeably different from Sis' tone.

"That better be Rob," I hear her yell from the living room.

"I don't know. I guess it's hard moving in and out," I reply.

"Well, you're always welcome back here any time," he says, leading me into the next room where dinner is waiting. "We could probably get you on at the plant," he continues, the notion planting a blade of fear into my skull.

"Thanks, Jack, I'll keep it in mind."

We step into the dining room where my younger brother and his wife are already seated with their two children. Joe stands up, gives me a hug, and introduces me to his ginger three-year-old. Sis is running back to the kitchen for a few condiments and extra plates.

Over the next hour I eat dinner while dodging conversations that dangle me from their centers. Joe wants me to go deer hunting, and Jack keeps inviting me to work at the plant. Joe's wife tells me she'll take me over to St. Clairsville to the new mall and get me a girl, while Sis campaigns for me to join their church. My own interests and activities are just something else, vague and different, not worth consideration. Around here people don't seem to realize that a person might not want the same things that they desire. More than anything, I'd say that's probably what made me leave.

We talk at the table about Pops in the past tense, as if he's already dead. By the time I step in the bedroom to see him again, I feel guilty for having a full stomach. Dad and I never had much in common, but I'd still like to talk and sense that feeling I get from him of an earlier generation, hear some old stories about how the town used to be.

I sit with him for half an hour on the wooden chair Sis has placed next to his bed, but after all the sitting I have nothing but a headache full of the family's conversations. The hardest part is to reconcile that there is no laughter left when a person gets to this point. I get up to go to the kitchen for something to drink. There's no need to offer Pops a Coke, peanuts, nothing.

When night falls, I feel like I'm in another world, a better one. There's really nothing better about it, maybe it's worse in fact, but it's an illusion I'm thankful for. I stop back at the hotel, shower quickly again, and plod over the bridge to the island. People consider islands romantic and tropical, but this one never landed on any magazine cover. There are some old mansions falling in on themselves here, other working-class homes soldiering on, the usual convenience store on the corner, and the same views as anywhere else of this steel factory river town.

I walk down to the end of the island to the casino telling myself I might try to go in and enjoy myself, but when I get there I'm as turned off as always. The parking lot seems as long as Main Street itself. There are even some tour buses from as far as Cleveland and Columbus parked in it. The pair of palm trees on the overhang to the entrance is as far as I can go before deciding to turn around and take the quiet walk back to the bridge. I don't mind the gambling, but I can't take all the fluorescence and lipstick.

I cross the bridge again, feel it shake a bit in the dark, and wonder when the mammoth was last inspected. I think about the engineering and labor that built this rainbow of steel arching through the sky. Between my feet, through the grid, the muddy water flows below. I reach the other side and continue on to Market Street before remembering the joints I saw earlier in the morning.

One can never tell if these places are open, closed, or out of business until seeing if anyone's breathing inside. What it is that makes me select the King's Alley over the V.I.P. Nightclub I'm not sure, maybe just the aqua-colored door. When I open it, I see a claustrophobic bar with the carpet removed and other renovations left undone, a loud television hanging in the corner. There is a small group seated together at one of the booths, and a man hunched at the bar under the bartender's conversation. Two females at the booth stop their conversation to look at me, so I sit down at the bar with my back to them and order my usual Old Crow. The bar stool feels new, but everything else is probably forty years old or more.

I focus on the whiskey and try to hunch over like the man two stools down, but I haven't been in this town or bar long enough to do it the same way. After a few sips, two more men enter—factory workers. They take their places at the bar to continue the mission they've started elsewhere. I remain quiet. I'm not here for conversation or community, just a warm place to feel lonely.

One of the men tries to start a conversation with me, but I'm bored with his slobbering before the first sentence is out. The two women from the booth get up from their stations to pet him, maybe just their way of closing in on me for all I know, but that's the last thing I need.

When the twenty-year-old walks in, greeting the bartender and pulling down her umbrella from the rain that's started again, something deep inside me says it's my turn. She's frisky on arrival, too talkative, and that sets off a strained mix of repulsion and attraction. I squint to take a closer look at her, from her hair and nose down to her wrists, her long legs, her red shoes.

"Haven't seen you here before?" she asks, bending her words just the right way as she sits down beside me, pulling out a cigarette.

"Yeah, I've been gone for a couple years," I answer, bringing her volume down a few notches, thinking that might make whatever passes between us more private.

"Back from Iraq, huh?"

"That where it was?" I ask, happy to see her using some kind of logic.

She laughs. We move on to the usual small talk, and I offer her a drink before the real flirting begins. I lose track of what's going on around me in the bar, concentrating on my drinking and on some illusion of pleasure that sits at my side. In her eyes and wit I sense potential. Once upon a time this girl was a princess, or one day she'll be in a better place, I'm sure someone has said. Romanticize the past and the future, but the present is a slump of profanity.

I take her back to the hotel, wondering what ghosts sleep in the deserted buildings we pass. She's not upset we have to walk, and it gives us time to negotiate a price.

"Sorry to be so commercial about it," I say.

"Don't sweat it, that's business," she says, trying to appear casual, but I see the nervousness coming through.

"Been doing this long?" I ask her, trying to believe I might talk one of us out of it, maybe even reach a legitimate friendship instead, my usual naiveté.

"Why do you ask me a stupid question like that? You know there's no work around here. It's not like where you been, where you get paid to fight."

"Yeah, I know. What the hell's going to happen to this town anyway?"

"Nothing's going to happen. It's always the same," she says. "I'm saving up and getting out before I'm too old to hope anymore."

I wonder what her plans might be, how much she wants to save and how long it'll take, where she'd like to go, what she'll do when she gets there, and how often she'd come back, if ever, but before I can ask any of my questions, we're at the hotel.

"You want to walk down to the river for a little bit or head on up?" I ask.

"What do you think? I don't have all night." At the bar she was a tease, but now we're on bricks and mortar with maybe a grenade or two.

We start to climb the stairs, but soon she's nearly out of breath. I put my hand into my pocket, fiddle with the key, and wonder if I should just drop it over the railing into the bushes. Her steps at the top are deliberate and labored, but that doesn't stop the key from gleaming in the moonlight.

Inside, things don't take long, not much longer than it takes to prepare instant coffee or get your burger at the McDonald's drive-thru. I pay her first and then put my conscience on hold, play on instinct, and convince myself the girl under me is only in my imagination. Then I just try to get this lust out of my loins so it doesn't come back.

She wants a shower before going back out to look for more, so I get her a clean towel and tell her to help herself. She walks to the bathroom and maybe forgets me. After I hear the shower turned on I reach over to the nightstand and dip into her purse to pull out her ID: Diane McFaddin. This takes me back to Don, my high school friend, and I stuff everything back inside, return the purse to its original spot. I can even remember the month almost twenty years ago when old Don passed around the cigars. I get up and turn the music back on, wonder if he ever thinks about what I'm doing these days. I hope to God he doesn't right now.

Out on the balcony the suspension bridge rises and lurks, beauty from 1849. The Ohio churns beneath it, and now I wonder if it is carrying the filth into town or away from it, maybe just mixing it altogether. I'm not sure there is anything left inside of that water to clean us all again. Instead, I see creeks full of two-headed frogs and turtles.

I turn back to sit on the bed and stare at the television. Don's daughter comes out of the bathroom five minutes later, looking the same as when she sat the umbrella down inside King's Alley, except now I see her father's dark eyes turned back at me. She doesn't need to say bye to me, just picks up her purse in stride. "It's a nice day for a white wedding" rings the chorus as the door slams.

I wake mid-morning, mildly hungry, but in no hurry. I'd like to sleep longer, but I don't want anyone to come looking for me. If there was a dead body in the floor next to my bed, I doubt I'd feel any differently. At least then I'd know what I was guilty of. But I get up, go back into the shower again, and find her hair stuck at the drain. I start to recall some of the kids who graduated with me and wonder what they might be doing now, wonder what I'd feel if one of them screwed my daughter. I shave, comb, and dress, turning my thoughts to when I might be able to leave this town again.

Outside, I lock the door to my hotel room and lean over the railing, look down at the parking lot while taking in some air. The space in my stomach has grown stronger. I could go to the house for breakfast, but I'd rather go back to the diner, take my chances that I'll be alone there. On the walk I feel like the morning fog that often hangs over the river.

At the diner I get my cup of coffee and order exactly what I had yesterday, down to the grape jelly. I eat until the plate is clean, get an additional order of sausage. A strong stomach is in my genes; otherwise, I'd already have ulcers. I ask for a last cup of coffee while I wander through the different scenarios of Dad's dying. Would it be better if he died now or hung on for a few months? Could I have done something differently during his life that would make me grieve now when I think of his death?

Maybe I'm stalling or maybe I've made a decision. I return to the hotel and a lobby clerk meets me as I begin to ascend the stairs, asks me if I'm staying another night. I don't stop or answer, just continue up to the third floor and enter my room. I go to the restroom, pack up all my useless items: Q-tips, plastic razors, a bar of Irish Spring, Old Spice deodorant, my toothbrush and my Colgate. Then I pick up the dirty clothes, wrap them up together, and put them back in my bag. I zip the bag and set it on the bed, ready to go.

Cars line the curb in front of the house when I finally make my slow walk over. It wouldn't take a dollar-store clerk to know my father is dead. On the porch I sit back down in one of the rockers. I start at a good pace and look out at the cloudy day. Something in the air is gone, but things won't change. Death will put an end to this town soon enough, but until then, this is how it's going to be.

The minister from Dad's church is the first to find me on the porch, shake my hand to introduce himself and offer condolences, then crack his whip fifteen seconds later. He starts his talk on Jesus and salvation, but I tell him I've long had it memorized. I feel a little sympathy for him with one eye, but a lot of hatred with the other. There's a corpse in this house, this city. If there weren't so many of the living to turn me off, I could kneel down and say a prayer myself, but inside I'm lost and lean over and say a simple good-bye to Dad.

There's one daily bus traveling west, and I'm rushing to meet it like the war is over and I'm going home. Greyhound is a few minutes late today as usual, giving me the time to buy a ticket at the counter. I push the bus company's employee to write a little faster, fearful the driver will come and go and leave me here another day. The bus pulls up just after the ticket is put in my hand.

I'm the only person getting on at this stop and there are plenty of open seats. I move to the back of the bus and find an empty row. It doesn't take but a few minutes until we pull out and drive up Main Street past the courthouse. I take a last glance at the river.

I feel the plush cushion of the seat under me, and the engine called up for more energy. I stretch out and try to relax my body. A few more pushes on the accelerator and we enter the highway tunnel that cuts through Wheeling Hill leaving town. Lights poke out from its walls like lanterns inside a haunted house. Mountains carved out, we crawl through their tummies, hollowed, infesting their blood like pouring nail polish in Dad's Bible.

Dad is gone, only a shell remains. I think about the steel factories along the river, how they do the same to this land, their giant cylinders standing like kings and emptying toxic breath into the air.

I wish I could spit out some fumes of my own, clean out whatever's inside of me. I wish I could do more than leave my bag sitting in a hotel room—its balcony door open to the old bridge that first crossed a mighty river, people settling at its feet.

GREENER GROUND

A cloudy week, yet Lester's face was sunburn red as he squeezed between cars in his cluttered garage. For many mornings he had held his breath, sighing in relief each time he saw that his early spring sodding wasn't in vain. Today, however, hopes for his front lawn's emerald glow showed its first signs of faltering. Small, circular patches of dead-brown grass had started to form in the July heat.

"I knew they were back," Lester fumed over the sound of television and running water as he entered the house, his veins stretching out like roots across his neck. "I'll never beat them," he growled, breathing heavily.

His wife Margaret stood at the kitchen sink, still in her pink robe. She turned off the water and peered across the living room at her husband's frustration. "What did you say, honey?"

"I said I'm tired of getting all of Versie's messes."

Dalton sat on the faded sofa with his favorite Power Rangers blanket, his father's tension interfering with an old episode of Scooby Doo. With sleep still in his eyes, his uncombed blond hair stood straight up.

"What are you going to do then, dear?" Margaret prodded, her eyes narrowing with concern. "You going to spray again? You've already sprayed so much stuff on that poor lawn."

"I don't know. I'm fed up. Ought to go over and spray Versie herself is what I ought to do."

"Now don't do that, Lester. You know she'll tell every soul out at church."

"Well, that's about the only thing I know to fix this once and for all. Hardly ever rakes her leaves, never trims the branches growing onto our property, old fence keeps leaning over...but this one, this beats all I've ever seen."

73

"You sure it's not something else?"

"I'm sure!" Lester roared, the question angering him further. He leaned over Dalton's head and picked up the phone to call his neighbor three houses down.

"Who you calling?" Margaret asked. Lester didn't respond.

"Hello, Charlie? Yeah, Lester Roudebush here. Listen, sorry to call you this morning, but I think I got them old chinch bugs again. Would you mind coming over to take a look sometime today when you can?"

Charlie spoke loudly, even louder than Lester, and Margaret could hear him through the telephone.

"Sure, Les, I'll come over right now if you want. I told you they were tough to get rid of. Get you some Sevin this time or they're gonna eat up your whole lawn."

"Yeah, guess I have to, Charlie. But they're coming from over at Versie Whitaker's I think. Well, I'll just see you in a bit and we'll go from there. Sure appreciate it." Lester hung up the phone with a racket and ignored his wife's next question, rushing back to his lawn.

Outside, Lester stood in the driveway, his hands stuffed into the frayed pockets of his khaki work pants as he looked dejectedly down at his lawn. He was trying with little success to get his fight back up and shake off the despondency when Charlie arrived holding an empty Folgers can—lidless and with its bottom cut out.

"You out of coffee, Charlie?" Lester asked.

"No, no, this is just a little trick I'm gonna show you, Les."

"Like to put it around old Versie's neck," Lester said with an ugly scowl. "If she wasn't the worst gossip at our church I'd go over there right now."

"I know it, Les, but let's take a look and make sure of what you got first." Charlie walked his large frame over to the lawn for a general inspection, mouth hanging open and years of working at Feed, Seed, and Weed in his pocket. He removed his glasses to kneel near the dying spots. His eyes were beady without them, like two marbles that might drop and fall into an open hole below. "Well, this is the season and these browning patches look just like them. Fix me up a bucket of soapy water and we'll see what you got here, Les."

Lester turned and walked quickly to the garage. Moments later he returned with a faded, yellow pail half-filled with sudsy water.

"All right, let's stick this can into the sod at the edge of these dead areas and then we'll pour in that soap and water," Charlie directed as he crouched down. "If you got any chinch bugs they'll rise up to the surface in a few minutes. Works on mole crickets, too."

Lester bent over to pour the soapy water into the container and then the two men stood up, staring at the brown spots in the middle of green as they waited for results. Margaret came out the front door and stood watching from the porch. Hands on hips, Lester repeated the foul words in his mind: chinch bugs. He thought how they rolled from Charlie's nasal voice like odd sounds from a babbling toddler.

"It's early July now, Les," Charlie said, interrupting his friend's thoughts. "If it's them chinch bugs and you don't do nothing it'll only get worse. I've seen them eat up an entire lawn in no time. Voracious."

"I'll go get me some of that Sevin today like you said."

"You better. It's a lot stronger than that stuff you've been using. Got that carbaryl discovered by Carbide in the 1950s."

"It's a good thing," Lester chimed. "Have to get them before they get you."

"Yep! Look here, Les," Charlie called out. "You got them all right. See them coming up to the top?" Lester's face grew sheepish, white birch pallor. "And you got the nymphs too."

"The what?"

"Nymphs. Babies. Them red ones. Problem is, Les, you can spray that Sevin until you are blue in the face, but if Versie's got them they'll be back unless she sprays, too."

"Lord, have mercy," Lester said, scratching his head. "Getting Versie to care for her lawn is like trying to milk a bull." Charlie worked hard not to laugh. "Why don't they crawl in some other direction?"

"Les, they ain't walking over here. They're flying."

"You're not serious, Charlie. You mean they fly?"

"Why sure they fly! I tell you, if I was you, I'd walk over there and just take a peep at Versie's lawn, see how it looks."

"Oh, hers is worse than mine, Charlie. I've already seen it. Her lawn's patchier than a hobo's jacket. That's how I know where they're coming from. Well, that and everything else wrong with my lawn starts with her."

"That don't sound good, Les," Charlie replied.

"Well, listen," Charlie finally said after the conversation went in circles for almost ten minutes, "I've got to get into town for some fishing equipment so I'm going to head out of here." At word of Charlie's departure, Margaret skedaddled back inside the house.

"Okay, Charlie. Sure. Thanks a bushel for your help."

Seconds after Charlie pulled out of the driveway, Lester jumped in his Ford Ranger speeding off to Feed, Seed, and Weed. He gripped the steering wheel and glared at the road like an enemy, arriving at the lawn care center in a quick fifteen minutes. In the parking lot he began dry rubbing his hands and scurried around rodent-like until he entered the store and found an aisle full of Sevin.

With three containers of concentrate, Lester marched to the checkout line. Behind two other customers he readied his cash impatiently, then, with a nod from the cashier, stepped up to the counter. He replied to the cashier's questions with short, hurried answers, counting out the money as he handed it over. Sevin paid for and in hand, he returned home still in a rush, not even collecting his receipt.

Dalton stood outside with a Nerf football hoping for a playmate when Lester arrived. One glance told him his father wasn't a candidate. Lester moved to the garage like a threatened animal. He rinsed out his sprayer and filled it half with water, then opened the Sevin and slowly added equal parts pesticide, the strongest ratio recommended. After screwing on the lid, he pressurized the sprayer and adjusted the nozzle to a narrow spray. Darting to the front lawn, he spent the next hour liberally applying the pesticide.

When finished, Lester went inside the house satisfied and grabbed a can of Coke from the refrigerator. He returned outside to drink and found Dalton fumbling with his football in the yard. "Dalton, get out of that grass! I just treated it!" Lester yelled. "Put that football away and go ride your bike somewhere." Dalton ran obediently to the garage, grabbed his bike, and peddled off. Lester took another long swig.

Across the street Clint exited his front door, preparing to mow his own lawn. Lester figured that he would go over and have a quick chat to fill him in on the chinch bugs, leaving out the part about Versie. Afterwards he would go inside for some lunch and then call a couple of friends, repeat the story until fatigued.

*   *   *

It was after midnight when Versie woke up and realized she had forgotten to take her reflux medicine, the acid already doing backflips in her chest. Reaching over to the nightstand for a light, her hand touched the wig that Dolores had bought her just before she began chemo treatment. Her fingers followed up the lamp's pipe until finding its knob. Versie turned on the light, then brought her hand back to settle on her chest. She stood up and reached over to the chair for her robe and put it on, her stomach none too settled either.

Versie's frame of eighty years creaked as she moved down the hallway, passing the room where her only daughter slept. Dolores had moved back home several years ago after divorcing. It upset Versie at the time, but now she tensed up at the thought of not having her daughter to rely on at home during cancer treatment.

Slowly she descended the steps and crossed the foyer on her way to the kitchen where she had all her medications laid out on the table. Walking by the large bay window that looked out over the front yard she glimpsed the movement of a shadow and faint light outside. Moving closer, she strained to catch a ghost-like image of a man. Hunched over and wearing a helmet light, the figure paced the lawn with a large canister in his hands. Versie jumped, momentarily imagining her deceased husband before her illusion gave way to worry. She told herself to go upstairs and wake her daughter, but before she could move, the man crept between two evergreens at the edge of the lawn and disappeared. Versie stayed at the window and stared into the darkness, the acid collecting in her throat.

Margaret awoke when Lester lifted the sheet and crawled back into bed. "You feeling bad, too, dear?" she asked.

"Just taking an Alka-Seltzer, honey," he replied, his smirk unseen in the darkness.

"Maybe them old chemicals making you sick again, Lester. I still smell them on you and you've been coughing since dinnertime."

"I'll be all right. Gotta make sure those chinch bugs take a hike."

"Dalton was vomiting you know."

"Well, I figure that may have just been old cheese he ate, Margie," Lester replied. "That dairy is finicky. Dalton will be all right, don't you worry. Now let's get some sleep."

*　　　*　　　*

Early Sunday morning Lester surveyed his lawn with a tiny smile. His eyes scanned the grass as if reading an official document awarding him a pay raise. He thought nothing of the numerous dead bees he found on the driveway or the mole lying on its back in the road.

At Grace Baptist that morning, Lester was the first to rise for testimony. "I'd just like to ask you all for your prayers in a little matter that's been ongoing in my life," he said, holding firmly onto the lapels of his navy blue sport coat as he spoke. "I believe and sure hope this problem has been fixed once and for all, but I just ask that it be done in Jesus' name." He paused as members of the congregation said amen. "Now it's nothing financial really. Or health related. But, well, all things are seen by God and I just put it in his hands."

Lester sat back down in his seat in the wooden pew, and Margaret patted him softly just above the knee. Brother Parsons the choir director launched into an impromptu verse of "Blessed Assurance," and Lester stood back up with the congregation.

After the singing, a loud chorus of amens echoed in the sanctuary as Lester and the rest of the congregation took their seats again. Only one parishioner remained standing—off to the side, in the back of the church. It was Versie Whitaker, gripping the back of the pew in front of her with both hands. At first much of the congregation didn't hear the faint and unsteady voice coming from the rear. But then her left hand let go of the pew and slowly rose to her temple. When she pulled the wig back from her bare skull, Lester wasn't the only one who knew she had a lot to say.

MANNEQUINS

Blue veins shot up from the sidewalk's ice. The morning had brought a storm that blanketed the entire region, and by evening the bricked, pedestrian-only streets were empty, caked with piles of sugar and sheets of glass. A pair of lone Mephisto boots slid over them now with a walk lacking confidence, tired from pressing down on the accelerator most of the day. Cheap shop windows of bygone buildings stared at his passing, as though reaching for a friend more than a customer.

Despite town hall's attempts at renewal, the Queen City of the Alleghenies, city of spires, looked much better from Highway 68 than it did from down inside its belly. Yet he didn't need smooth architecture, having stopped only in the hope that Shelly might be around to give him a space on the floor for the night. When he arrived at his ex-girlfriend's apartment building unannounced, however, no tugs on the loose door handle or straining of his eyes through cobweb-cornered windows made her appear. All he got for his knocking was pigeon shit on his palms from the window sills. If it wasn't wintertime, he'd sleep in his car. But he wasn't going to fight the roads anymore, so Shelly's absence would cost him ninety bucks, Holiday Inn style.

At half past ten, out on the streets again after checking-in, he knew the family had finished opening all the gifts under the tree. His weren't there—they sat cold in the back seat of his car, warmed only by cheap paper from McCrory's. He didn't mind missing out. Only duty had made him persevere since morning, beyond what safety recommended, but in the end the ice prevented his wheels from getting back home. He considered stopping in Pittsburgh to catch the train to Martinsburg, but fallen trees halted Amtrak as well. Despite his efforts he would catch hell for not getting home a day earlier, before the storm: his mother a sharpshooter when it came to applying guilt.

Lights from Christmas ornaments and street lamps refracted off the ice and snow, producing a cryptic glow across the old town. With all businesses closed, including McDonald's, not even a panhandler waited outside. People would say there was no reason to be out in these conditions, but he thought it a far better time and place to take a walk than through the thick air of other people's trite, mall conversations. He reached inside the camouflage jacket that blended in with nothing of his current predicament and pulled out a small bottle of Old Grand-Dad won at his plant's holiday gift swap. He took a big pull of the whiskey, then inhaled deeply and sent out a smoky heat.

Across the river, on the side of town where a fort once stood as a frontier outpost during the French and Indian War, a hazy mix of elaborate mansions stood under a moonlit sky. The storm, the holidays, and general decline of the town joined together to bring about a strange atmosphere: a ghost town bright and radiant even as midnight perched on vacant buildings around each lost corner. The moon hung over the hill in front of him, a glow-in-the-dark, light green fuzz behind the clouds.

He didn't expect any optimism, but he felt a dusty urge to call home again. Mother picked up after the fourth ring and speared scorn through his ear.

"Ain't no reason for you to keep calling, Dennis," she said, clearing her voice and half-choking. "The kids already done opened all their packages but yours. You ain't here and we're getting ready for bed."

"You still smoking, Mom?" he asked. She didn't answer and he backtracked. "Ma, I just wanted to call and see how everything went."

"Boy, you really are something ain't you? I told you to come in yesterday, but you always think you know better than us. Been expecting this storm all week, but smart old Denny thinks he can outfox the weather."

"I told you, Ma, I couldn't get off work any earlier or I would have left before this morning. I'm in Cumberland now, so I'll see you all early tomorrow."

"I ain't so sure you can get in here tomorrow neither the way them roads are looking. But you're going to do whatever you're going to do I reckon."

"All right, Ma. Well, I hope you all had a good time opening gifts. Jimmy put on a good show?"

"Dennis, I'm going to bed now. Jenny'll tell you all about it if you get here. She ain't leaving until Sunday. You know some children come in and stay a whole week."

"All right then, Ma. Good night."

He closed his phone and wondered, as he did at some point every year during his holiday headache, how going home once a year for a few days could cause such tension. *Will it be any easier when Mom dies?*

The silence of the town grew stronger. He looked around to see if someone was hiding in the doorway of a shop or standing against the corner of a building, but the only eyes belonged to mannequins in a nearby shop front. He stepped up to the window of the hand-me-down jewelry and clothing store to peer inside. The mannequins stood tall and full-figured, their skin unblemished. Decorated with plastic beads and second-hand scarves, a few returned his gaze, but most stared into space. All held calm and contented faces like no one at home could do. Maybe because the mannequins had no ideas of their own, no interest or ability to exert any influence or experience, no stress. They were all cross-eyed: most only slightly, but one or two considerably. *Would he trade his excellent eyesight for their serene demeanor?*

The snow continued to fall, flakes slipping down behind his collar onto the nape of his neck. Fiery like his late father who always preferred cold to heat, he let them sit on his skin like icy pinpricks, melting where they landed. He turned from the storefront and looked back in the direction of the Holiday Inn. If only a bar was open.

He found his own tracks in the white powder. They had grown fainter as the hour passed and it continued to snow. He followed the faint steps for ten minutes and arrived back at the hotel. There were still only five vehicles in the parking lot and his car had the least accumulation of piled snow. Walking behind his '88 Plymouth, he rubbed the snow away from the keyhole to open his trunk. After pulling out a second bottle of his favored whisky, banner year at the Christmas gift exchange, he slammed the hood shut and watched the disturbed snow scatter into a mist. Bottle in hand, he turned and walked to the hotel entrance.

Inside, the lone hotel clerk sat behind the counter in her uniformed grey blouse and blue skirt. She perked up when the door opened, greeting him with the customer service polish that made him want to sneak past unnoticed. The lobby was compact, even tighter with the Christmas tree and decorations, and with so few people at the hotel he knew he'd need to find that corner of his mind where he stored small talk.

"Happy holidays," she said with a lipsticked grin, tapping her manicured nails on the counter.

He caught her cheery demeanor and feared she might expect the same from him. "Nobody else shown up yet, right?"

"How did you know?"

"Still only five cars in the lot."

She peered at his face, taking her time to try and read it. "Ah, Christmas clever," she said, replanting her smile. "There's your car, my car, a businessman who got stuck here, and another couple. Don't even know who the truck could belong to. There isn't a store open in the whole town."

He wasn't too adept at reading between such lines, but he got the feeling she was trying to flirt. "You here all night?" he asked, recognizing his mistake as the words left his mouth.

She tilted her head and narrowed her eyes. "Until seven in the morning. How about you?"

He told himself to make sure she understood he wasn't interested. "Well, I need to get back home sometime tomorrow. Family's waiting on me." Family might mean a wife and kids, he figured, turning towards the elevator.

"Where's home?" she asked, not letting him depart so easily.

"Tomahawk, West Virginia," he answered, turning back to face her. He paused, telling himself not to reciprocate, but she didn't need it.

"I just moved here six weeks ago from Chicago. Husband got transferred and I'm still trying to adjust."

She had been saving this up to tell someone, maybe everyone, but at least she was married, and he had read her friendliness and body language all wrong. He wanted to tell her she should get over her anxiety: moving to Cumberland wasn't like getting dropped to fight in the Syrian Desert. Instead, he just repeated the word Chicago three times, she could make of it what she liked, and then he told her he was going up to make a cup of coffee. He expected a quick "good night" and turned to the elevator a second time.

"Make it good and strong," she said, her laughter exploding toward his ear, burning him in the back.

He didn't wait for the elevators and bolted for the stairs. Exiting the stairwell on the fifth floor, he turned left, then doubled back past the stairs, his room just to their right. He took out his plastic key, inserted it in the slot, and the sensor lit up green. Inside his room he removed his jacket and sat on the bed momentarily before deciding to start his coffee, thinking of home again, or what used to be home. Five minutes passed before he stood up, fiddled with the coffee maker on the counter, and began sorting through the supplies—only one small packet of sugar.

He took the elevator back down to the lobby and the doors opened to find her standing beside the sofa, away from her spot behind the counter. She smiled when he reappeared, more than artificial glee. He admitted to himself that she was attractive, if only in professional appearance.

"That was a quick coffee!"

"There's no sugar up there."

"Oh, really?" she teased, shifting her weight to one hip.

"There's only one packet of sugar in my room," he rephrased. "Do you have a few more packets?"

"Let me check and see if I've got any back here," she answered more seriously, returning to her post. He followed her and heard her hands rummaging through papers and supplies behind the counter. "Don't see anything here. There must be some more sugar back in the restaurant though." She moved quickly into the lobby again, not surprising for a young person with energy to burn after sitting around too much. He put his hands in his pockets as she flashed past him. "Follow me back," she said. "You might have to help me look."

He followed her down the hall past the elevators to the dark opening of the restaurant that had closed several hours ago. She couldn't find the light switch on the wall and edged further into the darkness.

"I'll see if I can just find you a full container back here," she said, her voice trailing as she disappeared into the kitchen, leaving him to loiter around the restaurant tables.

As his eyes adjusted to the darkness, he found convenient packets of sugar on every table. He felt an urge to take something more than sugar: a saltshaker, salad bar container, anything used by this commercial endeavor. Since she was nearby, however, he settled for what he needed, putting several packets of sugar inside his pocket. By the time she returned, he had retreated closer to the entrance and considered leaving without her.

"Oh, I'm sorry it took so long," she said, holding out a plastic container to him filled with sugar. "I had to pour some into this for you. It's enough isn't it?"

"Yeah, it will be plenty," he said, reaching for the container, ready to leave.

Softly, slowly, with dexterity, she controlled how he took the sugar from her hand. She stopped talking for a moment and slipped closer to him. He turned away to the side, feeling an awkwardness wash over him like a mother's reprimand.

"I can't believe everything's closed," she said seductively. "You sure you don't need anything more than just a cup of coffee?"

His neck bent downwards until his eyes rested on darkened ground. He knew she was reading his reactions, staring at him, right at his jaw, just below the ear where a day of stubble had grown. He looked back up, knowing further delay might make the situation worse, give her the wrong idea. From the corner of his eye he could see her smiling, but in the darkness the shadows deformed her face and the eyes appeared as empty sockets. Her hair had lost its golden shine and looked like two large strands of rope falling from her neck.

He led her back out into the hallway before responding. "Think I might just fix me that cup of coffee and take another walk through town." He didn't wait for an answer, turned his back and walked over to the elevator, pushed the button.

She still wasn't in view when the doors opened and he turned around inside the elevator to face the lobby again. Through the lonely fog of his mind he thought of the sky outside: the moon and the glare from streetlamps and the snow all mixed their luster together in the dark cold, beams and crystals of light shining over dreary life.

THEIR EVENING WALK

She closed the back door as dusk hovered behind the ridgeline, a darkness ready to swoop. They were late, she knew, and didn't want to go, hesitant to walk back where the trees would be shadows waving their bones, inviting her to some other place.

But he told her they wouldn't linger—and that she needed the exercise. "We'll just walk to the overlook and come back. You can make it that far, can't you?"

And she agreed, for he had already picked up his cane.

He replayed his early afternoon phone conversations to himself as they left the driveway, walking down the subdivision's dead-end street where the fields and forested mountainside held out against eviction. The neighbors had turned off their sprinklers, and streaks of red washed the sky behind the houses. After three telephone calls he still didn't believe it was the right voltage regulator, but the vendor who stocked Lucas parts insisted it was the correct four-terminal connection. At least she hadn't disturbed him all afternoon, allowed him to scan his MG club magazines and make his calls. She hadn't even asked if he wanted milk with his tea, just brought it to him on a little tray after his dinner of leftover pork chops and potatoes.

She stepped over the low chain someone had hung many years ago at the end of the road. Off the pavement the land angled downwards and headed for wild. Transferring her weight from concrete to soil brought a grimace, a twinge from her injured ankle as it came down on a rock, an acorn under the leaves, maybe even something of archaeological significance. He could see that she came up lame. Yes, she had on her walking boots and had tightened the laces, she assured him as he looked down to double-check and reiterate the necessity of ankle support.

"Should've looked more closely where you were stepping then. You know how them rocks grow around here."

She mumbled, but he didn't hear, and she let it die—the idea that they moved too fast—knowing even a haw of skepticism could bring forth his rambling...twenty minutes about the boots and proper footwear, preparation, appropriate considerations. Instead, she put her weight on the foot and walked a circle: nothing serious, nothing to talk about. Carry on.

So they made their way downhill, past those maple trees standing with more pride and confidence than ballroom dancers, their arms swaying in bright red and yellow dresses, burning, with dancing fever. A blanket of leaves covered their steps as they walked cautiously, limiting faith. And into the field, flatland—the perfect spot for another residential lot, he often said. With his talk and sundown sowed in her mind, she thought how men used the bodies of the trees, how they cut them down, chopped, trimmed, and filed to make something to their own glory.

Squirrels roamed the ground and busied themselves with acorns, their operative, skeletal hands working like little men: rubbing them together over a fire, gloating over a deal, ready to bury small bags of money. Her father had once picked the little mammals up off nearby mountainsides, bulleted for their brains and a little meat, and she wondered where they went to die if not plucked: high up in their nests or in some faraway field, forgotten, while their children scampered about, flicking their tails?

She watched how he leaned on the crook-handled walking stick that his great-great-grandfather carried from Nelson County over the Shenandoah Valley, deep into the mountains. Four generations had passed down the solid oak staff, and he had used it with increasing frequency since retirement, its three-inch ferrule and original dark varnish still fine. "It ain't for support. It's in case of them damn dogs or anything else," he had told her many times with a fervor that seemed to want a wild boar, black bear, maybe mastodon.

"You take your medicine?" she asked.

He stopped, spoke in a low voice as if channeling all that had wandered the hills. "I told you once. I'll not say it no more."

He thought of his '68 MG again, this one racing green, the third he'd reconstructed in the last five years. No, he'd never convert the car's wiring to a three-terminal connection—it would sit until he found the original. "You talk to Janet about watering the plants and feeding Nixon if I go over to Lynchburg on Monday to get them parts?" he asked, making plans.

"No, I didn't get a chance." She wouldn't say he had occupied the phone for most of the afternoon.

"Well, you better make sure she ain't visiting her daughter in Nitro this week. Otherwise, I'll have to go by myself and you'll miss out on that little bakery. Man over there swears it's what I've been looking for."

"I'll call her this evening," she answered, thinking how she'd order two custard-filled donuts and an Earl Grey.

They walked past the field and onto the wide path leading deeper into the woods. The sun had fallen into the trees cascading down the mountainside. Birds chirped and prepared to roost.

"Yeah, better call her. I'm raking the yard tomorrow and leaving on Monday."

She looked at his free hand where the stump of his index finger ended at the knuckle. "Best thing that could have happened to me in Pusan," she overhead him say on the telephone at least once a year. She envisioned the gun, now just a rake, in his veiny hands—the long pole tightly gripped as its teeth dragged dried leaves across the front lawn into small piles, brown in death. Bagged and dumped over the hillside, but they would return, blow in, cover the ground anew after he came inside the house to wash off and sit down with ice tea. She looked again at the cane—how its smoothed wood supported a barrel-chested man whose skin had tightened around his bones, how he used it to tear up the wild mushrooms they came across during their walks. And she imagined what might transpire now if he ever had to use it in self-defense. Would he wave it intensely, lose balance and fall? What came after protection but swing after swing without forbearance?

"Don't suppose you've heard from Lil, have you?" he asked. "Been over a week."

"Haven't talked to her since the surgery. She don't want to say much."

He didn't answer. No news, no discussion.

"I just hope they don't try to have another one. It's awful. Might be Downs too, I don't care what that doctor says."

He cut her off. "Be still, you're just speculating. Leave it alone or you'll be back in the hospital. They'll move on with their lives and you'll be stuck in a little room eating TV dinners and making yourself crazy again."

The path had narrowed and their gait slowed as they ascended a hill. She heard a scratching, a scurrying in the undergrowth a few feet away, and she jumped, her neck twitching. Unlike him, she believed anything might show up in the woods.

Her nervousness made him grip his walking stick tighter. "We're turning 'round just up ahead," he said. She knew he meant where the trail ended at a cliff overlooking the valley, a view of more mountains rising on the other side of the interstate, watched by a petroleum bulk station. They often rested there before returning home.

"Yeah, I reckon I'll pay him about whatever he asks if he's got what he says he's got."

But she had left him—the jargon, the parts. Whatever it was he needed, her eyes watched for what floated between the trees branches.

At the top of the hill a clearing exposed an outcrop of limestone stitched with moss and lichen. He led, climbing up the white mass using his cane to balance. At the top, he put his hands on his waist and took in a deep breath. He looked out at the hills and down at the river sliding alongside the highway.

She followed him up, her ankle stressed again, and felt the tightness of her boot rubbing the corn of her little toe. Standing next to him, a breeze brought her the smell of the Kentucky Club tobacco in his clothes, and she thought of home, of freeing her feet—except first they'd have to walk back through the woods, the field, under the last trees, and finally the road. They'd arrive to blackness on their front porch—a blackness confident and relaxed in her rocking chairs.

Inside the house he'd turn on the lights. She'd turn on lights. And more lights. And they'd separate, to different rooms. She'd remove her boots, perhaps even go to the bathtub to soak her varicose-veined feet, the toes scrunched from wearing shoes far too small throughout her rural Clay County childhood. She might not see him again until a plate of bacon sat on the breakfast table.

"That ankle holding up?" he asked. "Better get you some Epsom salt when we get back."

Yes, she knew darkness was descending as he turned from the overlook and repeated they wouldn't tarry. Words unchanging, firm as death. She let him climb down first, of course, her life deferred.

As he slowly made his way down onto the narrow path towards home, she looked at the back of his head and the little crook at its base, a skull reminding her of the limestone rocks on which she stood. And from above she pondered what a walking stick might do.

THE COUGAR

"Cougar on the Loose" read the headline in Coalburn's weekly, although even the hardest of hearing were already in firm possession of the news. Fay Tomblinson read it again as her thin frame fidgeted in the rocking chair on the front porch of her inherited Victorian mansion. The words finally made her a believer too. Yes, she had overheard Gideon telling Mr. Felton about it one morning at the pharmacy, listened while Mrs. Kaufman warned customers at the mid-week farmers market, and even received word of the animal as recently as yesterday afternoon by her own hairdresser, but still she couldn't imagine any truth in it.

"Let people talk, but I'll not be fooled by their malarkey," she had said to Tully Barnett. "There aren't any cougars in these hills. But those wildfires of hot air, Tully, now there's still plenty of them to go around. Old gossip's stuck in every coat pocket and sidewalk crack."

But it was true, not idle chatter after all, and Fay took the better part of an hour to make her way through the article. She had been a methodical reader her whole life, eyesight still exceptional, but now she paused almost with each paragraph, closing the paper to imagine the cougar: its pointy teeth, the sharpness of its claws, the question of its origins. Then looking out over the ten acres of property founded by her grandfather, one of the three coal barons who established their small town, she thought of the grandchildren in Chicago, the wasp nest under the eave, the rotting apples in the front yard—mercy, she couldn't collect all of them. The monthly town hall meeting was only days away, and so the cougar would be the big news. *The cougar! What to do about it?* She took a sip of lemonade to settle her mind before reopening the newspaper.

When she finally finished the article, Mackendoyle Brogan stood at her gate like a young boy on stage waiting for his cue, greasy handed as usual. Fay wondered how the auto mechanic timed things so impeccably, not to mention how her niece's husband had the rosy cheeks of a toddler even as he neared fifty years of age.

"Goodness, Miss Fay! Guess that cougar's official now!"

"I think everyone already knew about that cougar. But come on in."

"Law, this ain't just everyone," Mackendoyle said, careful not to touch the immaculate white fence with his hands. "Now it's in the newspaper too!"

"I know it, Mack. Glass of lemonade?"

"No, no. I was just on my way to the post office. Got a couple things to drop off there. Paying bills as usual."

"So where in the world do you think this animal could have come from?"

"No idea. Been wondering myself. People done all kinds of figuring, but not a one of them makes much sense. I guess we'll get more answers in the paper next week."

"I doubt people will want to wait that long, Mack."

"You're right. Solomon Gun, Lester Koontz, and several others are already planning to go up the mountain to catch it. Folks even started placing bets."

"Well, it isn't Sasquatch, but I'd be careful if I was them. You aren't getting any crazy notions yourself are you?"

"Lord, no, Miss Fay. But somebody's gotta catch it. We got a scared community right now. Can't just let that thing run around here on its own terms."

"How far's it been coming in?"

"Oh, it's been right on the outskirts of town. Benny Crookshanks saw it coming down off the mountain behind Derwin Field's property."

"You're kidding me."

"No I ain't either. And Billy Drennen saw it on the other edge of town one evening after driving from the lumberyard. People say it looks real hungry, so it's only gonna get braver." Mackendoyle paused. "It's a bad omen, Miss Fay. Cougars ain't been around here since before we was born, back when they opened the mines. People are scared it'll pick up a child and carry it off. Ain't nothing a youngin could do. Come to think of it, not much to do if a cougar set its mind to picking up you or me neither."

"Let's try not to worry too much, Mack," Fay said, her sweaty palm securing the glass of lemonade. "That won't do us much good. I guess the sheriff has got his crew together and made some plans." She lifted the glass to her mouth and took a drink as Mackendoyle looked on enviously.

"Yeah, that's true. And supposedly the county is sending out its animal control services tomorrow, but even they've said people need to be real careful because catching that thing could take awhile."

"Maybe I'll just stay indoors until they do," Fay said with a little laugh to disguise her worry. "Lord knows I've done enough canning this summer to get me through three winters. Surely I can outlast a cougar."

Mackendoyle chuckled. "I reckon so. Well, listen, I better get a move on it and get these bills sent to their rightful places before they come looking for me."

Fay Tomblinson watched Mackendoyle wander off down the sidewalk, his pot-bellied, lanky frame passing behind an old sugar maple. His presence had given her some comfort, but now that he was gone a certain fear returned, one she'd tried to keep at bay since reading the headlines. She thought a moment longer, then picked up her empty glass and newspaper and walked inside the house. For the first time in years she locked the front door behind her.

Fay stepped off the front porch and slowly walked to her mailbox, wondering if Janice would indeed "come by around noon." She looked to one end of the street, then the other, but despite the pleasant weather saw no one outside. Even with a relaxing light wind stirring in late August, she went no farther, refused to take a much-desired walk around her property. She had even assigned Mackendoyle additional lawn work normally done herself.

"Don't worry. I'll take care of everything, Miss Fay," he had told her three weeks earlier. "Until that animal's caught and gone for good, just let me know what you need done."

She reached for the newspaper and read another Friday headline: "Day 27: Two More Sightings." Then she stuck her hand into the adjacent mailbox and took out financial statements, an electric bill, two pieces of junk mail, and a letter from Charles. Fay fiddled through the papers for a moment before lifting her head to look at her house. She glanced at the barn, then past the elm and maple trees towards a pile of firewood near the tire swing. This was still her property. Past the rhododendrons and dogwoods stood the house where both her father and grandfather had lived, but for several years she had felt a growing insecurity. What would become of the place? It should pass on to her son, or perhaps her daughter, but neither was capable of maintaining it. Charles would soon leave Chicago for San Francisco, and Janice didn't have the funds even to pay utilities. She was half-ashamed. Her own father wouldn't have allowed such a situation. No, Clarence Tomblinson wouldn't let a cougar run loose for more than a day either. Nothing that upset the stability and growth of the town, neither man nor beast, stood a chance against him.

Why couldn't they just kill the animal and return things to normal? She'd at least like to walk across her land again. The more she isolated herself from the grounds of her property, the more she contemplated her own mortality; not so much the dying part, but the almost inevitable loss of the land that had defined both her family and the town for generations. Who would care for the family cemetery out back? Who would remember Jacob Tomblinson, that young and venturous Scotsman who had risked everything coming down from Philadelphia? Who would remember the coal company he built from nothing, that vast success, the lifeline and authority for miles around? Would the name Tomblinson mean any more than the dust blowing on the new highway that bypassed town?

Fay spotted Lester Koontz crossing the street behind her. Lester wouldn't speak to her unless forced, so she kept her back turned and fingered the envelopes a moment longer. When she glanced back to make sure he'd gone, Jimmy Cobb appeared, practically in her face. Fay jerked.

"That cougar making you a little jumpy, Mrs. Tomblinson?"

"No, I think it's you that's making me jumpy, Jimmy."

"Ain't that what a good son-in-law is paid to do?" he asked, a lump of Mail Pouch showing like a tumor inside his cheek. Fay rolled her eyes and stepped inside her gate. "Anyway, Janice says she can't come over as planned."

"Oh? Why is that? You all have too many grocery sweepstake cards to etch off?"

"Well, her Paget's got real bad last night."

"So bad she can't pick up the phone?"

"I ain't real sure, Mrs. Tomblinson. She wanted me to tell

93

you before Lester and I head up into the mountains again to win that cougar bounty. Pot's up to a thousand."

"All right then, Jimmy," Fay replied, seeing no reason to prolong the conversation.

But Jimmy Cobb persisted. "Four legs can't just walk into our town like he owns it. Done scared enough people." He paused to snicker and spit. "And when we get it Lester says we're gonna put its stinking claws and teeth on the shop counter of Mr. Peace Lover himself."

"You mean Jerry Giles? Why in the world would you want to do that, Jimmy?"

"You know how much people hate him. Lester says that with all those books he owns he should know that this town was built on coal. Says it's always the people who ain't from around here that want to come in and say how everything should be if they can't own it themselves. That jackleg's even got out-of-state lawyers looking in on Appalachian Lumber now."

"So what if he does, Jimmy? What's the cougar got to do with any of this? I'm sure Appalachian Lumber has got their own lawyers."

"Well now he says we don't even need to kill that cougar. Just trap and release it. Lester says if that's going to be the case, he'd like to see ole' Giles trap and release it himself then."

"I think Lester and Lester's friends need to worry more about themselves and less about that fellow from Boston," Fay said before turning to leave.

"Say, I know I ain't supposed to ask, but did Janice get that Paget's from you or her daddy? I just thought it might be important somehow to know."

"Jimmy, why don't you go around back and ask my husband about that?"

"Now, Mrs. Tomblinson, I ain't no necromancer."

"Maybe not, but I'd imagine you'd like his answer a pretty puppy more than mine. Now tighten up that belt if you're going after that cougar."

Jimmy Cobb didn't answer, turned and left with two more spits of brown juice into the muddy ground.

Fay paused at the small section of birthday cards and looked up to see who had entered The Whole Bean. At noon she had realized her grandson's birthday had crept up on her and was only two days away. She called Mackendoyle to pick up a card for her at the Rite Aid in Bluefield, but he was busy under a customer's hood. Out of options, she decided to brave the block and a half to Jerry Giles' shop.

She steered her neck and saw her daughter scanning the store's message board for newly posted, part-time employment listings amidst the hand-scribbled notes for lost pets, pictures of used items for sale, and flyers on environmental awareness and vegetarianism. The herbal scents and smell of coffee refreshed Janice, and Fay decided not to approach her daughter. Instead, she returned the birthday card to its slot and took a few steps back to screen herself from view.

Jerry Giles' store was unique for Coalburn. Both a coffee shop and community education center as Jerry himself called it, the store sold books, baked goods, gifts, and homeopathic medicines. Jerry complained there wasn't enough support and business, but what did he expect? He had opened the store a little more than a year ago after moving into town, and plenty of people didn't trust him and his outspoken politics. Still, other than the pharmacy, his shop kept more customers than any store on Main Street.

"How are we doing, Janice?" Fay heard Jerry greet her daughter from behind the counter. "You look tired."

"Oh, you know, Jerry. The usual," Janice replied with a deep sigh.

Fay recalled how a few short months ago Janice was shy to say much to the out-of-town man who looked sophisticated even in a flannel shirt and beard. Now Fay believed Janice shared more information with Jerry than with her own mother.

"Did you stop taking that St. John's Wort I gave you?"

"No, no, still on it. Think it's my Paget's that's been getting worse."

"I see. Do you need some more calcium-rich herb mix? It couldn't hurt to double it."

"I might just do that, but got to wait until my next check comes."

Fay grimaced. She'd intended for months to bring up those herbal supplements with Janice.

"Then how about a cup of coffee? It's on me."

"I appreciate it, Jerry. Sure could use a pick-me-up."

"No problem. Just take me a minute. By the way, I know your doctor keeps telling you it's Paget's disease, but if I were you I'd check with someone who knows alternative medicine. You worked near the mines for twenty years and your body is full of its toxins."

Fay's face reddened. Jerry always talked down about the mines.

"Don't know if I could afford it, to be honest with you," Janice answered.

"It wouldn't cost much for a consultation. I know a couple of people not too far away who would give you a discount if you give them my name."

"Let me think it over then."

Jerry smiled big, then turned to make the coffee while Janice went back to the message board. "And I'm sorry, I almost forgot to tell you. Your mother came in just a few minutes ago. She must have left when I was in the back."

"I'm surprised, considering she doesn't go out much now. She's paranoid about that cougar. Seems like she thinks it's looking for her for some reason."

Jerry laughed. "That's funny. But people are saying it's the first in a century around here?"

"It's crazy, Jerry. Haven't been any in my lifetime. Just asking everyone to pray about it."

"Pray?" Jerry stopped and looked back at his customer.

"Well, the Lord saved Daniel from the lion's den so I suppose he can save Coalburn from a single cougar. Least I hope so," Janice replied with a slight giggle.

"I'm not sure it's best to wait on God to take control," Jerry countered.

"I know it, but it couldn't hurt for some of us to pray about it while others are out trying to kill it."

"Yeah, that's what I don't understand, Janice. Everyone is gung-ho on killing the poor animal. Where's the love in that? No one has to kill it. Just trap it and set it free where it won't bother people."

"These are hunting people around here, Jerry. You know that by now."

Jerry turned with the coffee in hand and a smirk on his face. "All right, Janice," he said, resigned to her point. "Here's some good coffee anyway. Enjoy."

Janice added cane sugar and organic milk, then took a sip. "Boy, Jerry. That's a strong cup!"

"Yeah, it's from the Ethiopian highlands. And I'm sure they don't go killing all their wildcats there."

Fay turned quietly for the restroom.

Evening came and the sun fell in bloody red as Fay stood at the kitchen sink. She stared through the window onto the back of her property and waited as her Alka-Seltzer dissolved. Janice had called to inform her about the recent medical procedures, told her it would take three days for the biopsy results. Fay thought what it would mean if the news was as bad as expected. The fizzing leapt from the glass into her mind. The sky itself appeared injured, and Faye Tomblinson imagined the beams of dying light breaking into specks and shards.

But did the light deceive her when the animal came into view, elegantly prowling across her land as if to explore a new purchase? Fay dropped her glass, its gassy liquid hissing as it fell into the sink, and her scream mixed fear, anger, and frustration, as if the cougar's appearance signaled the final stage of an unfixable catastrophe.

The animal stopped and turned to stare at the window as though it heard the elderly woman's cry. Its face grew larger, freezing Fay as she looked into its sleepy eyes. Fay thought she saw a sadness that mirrored her own, but simpler, as if the animal had finally grown tired of anger and lost expectations. The cougar took another step toward the house and hesitated, unsure of itself. Then it turned in the direction of the mountains, its head sinking toward the ground, moving gingerly.

Her own stare released by the animal's departure, Fay turned to the phone and punched the numbers in a panic. In her fear she again saw her property, how it would disappear and fade when she was gone, how her own children had either wilted at home or departed altogether. Mackendoyle picked up after the first ring.

"It's here, Mack. Right behind the house. That cougar. I'm calling the sheriff now. Get over here right away and tell anyone you can that I've seen it."

"The cougar? Okay, be right over, Miss Fay. You stay inside, you hear?"

As curious about people as he was automobile engines and cougars, Mackendoyle rushed out of his house. Ten minutes later he arrived to find Fay quiet and trembling, the telephone handset off its cradle. He picked the phone up and called the police department.

"Sheriff Loudermilk is out of town and won't be back until morning, Miss Fay, but I'll stay here with you awhile. And you know you're welcome to come stay with Mabel and me tonight if it makes things easier."

"Out of town? What about our town?" Fay asked, her voice loud, but quavering.

"I don't know, but have you thought about taking a little vacation, Auntie? You could go visit Charles for a couple of weeks or something. Couldn't hurt. That cougar is getting more and more desperate by the day and somebody's gonna get it soon. Might as well rest a little easier until it's done."

"I'm not leaving, Mack," Fay stated, her voice rising.

"Now, Miss Fay, I know Charles wouldn't mind."

"This is my property."

Mack knew better than to force the issue. Instead he fixed a pot of coffee and sat down at the table beside her. For over an hour they sat without saying much. The mechanic studied Fay's face for a sign, but his aunt's countenance looked drained, and her eyes were as lifeless as stone. Her only movement came from a tired breathing, and Mackendoyle Brogan watched as her chest would rise and fall, rise and fall.

Fay Tomblinson glanced at the window again, but darkness had come and there was nothing to see. She, too, could see the rise and fall, and searched for steady walls.

THROUGH THE HOLLOW

The hills are misty, shivering with color as the sun crawls over the ridge. When he's searching for ginseng, Cowley's the only other person I know who might tramp up this mountainside, but even he's not up here Sunday mornings, up here early like me to meet the sun before anyone can guilt me into the car for morning services.

When it hasn't rained and the footing is firm, it's only a twenty-minute hike up to the first jutting rock that's large and level enough to sit down upon. I stop there and take out breakfast, rip off a piece of cold, crusty-skinned chicken breast and put it into my mouth, chew slowly. Buttered bread washed down with a swallow of the first cup of tea from my thermos sends a chill over me in the October morning, tasting richer with the sweet smell of earth in my nostrils. Brown thrashers and grey catbirds flit as their bills rummage the soil, kicking up specks of dirt and dead leaves.

Through the fog I can make out home below, alongside the creek that twists with the road between the two mountains. Even with the fiery brilliance of autumn leaves, some kind of a persistent grey never goes away. And when the last leaves fall and dry up in the coming weeks, the hills will fill with skeletons: bony, brittle trees. I look down at the land and think how desperate people must have been to first crawl up in these hollows to settle.

Carpenter ants have started their drive towards me as I finish the tea and pack up my food case, trash, and thermos. I stand up and look down at the valley; in another hour exhaust fumes will be shooting from vehicles as they slide across the blacktop towards a grieving sanctuary, its congregation to pray for Mom again. All that prayer starts to blur, like the doctor's voice when he told us her cancer had spread. I walk another twenty minutes to the top of the mountain telling myself to forget it all: the mountains are

99

sacred, and I come just to clear my mind. Still, I can't help thinking how prayer in this hollow is mostly a Sunday activity while cancer works seven days a week.

That red fox runs as my eyes clear the ridge line where the land levels out and the trees thin. It's surprised again, having never learned my schedule. I stop briefly to rest in the quiet, then cross and move further down the ridge.

From the other side of the ridge, a few hundred yards on, I can see LBC Recycling Center down through the trees. I start my decline at an angle, watching each step so as not to turn an ankle. The recycling center is fenced off against trespassing, so if I don't come out beside it I'll need to retrace my steps back up the mountain until I get it right. Next to the recycling center is a private residence, and down off the mountain I follow the fence separating the two. Dogs growl as I walk quickly past the mobile home to reach the road.

Broken glass and empty automobile frames are strewn along the recycling center's long, narrow lot. What do the mountains think watching it each day? Materials sit in their own lonely places: rusted car parts, old refrigerators with jars of dill pickles trying to slide out, broken shovels and rakes missing teeth. Together they hide the buying and selling of stolen copper, the center's cash crop.

At the intestine-shaped road that runs a quarter mile into town I walk its shoulder to avoid the intermittent traffic. Saturday night's bar lovers have probably found a bed or the floor by now, but a revved-up car can shoot off this twisted tar quicker than a copperhead strikes an ankle. Even the preachers sometimes swerve recklessly onto the berm.

The mountains loom as I walk down the road, making the roofs of the trailers and houses that sit in the thin bottomland look like outhouses. Mr. Vance's house is probably the most coveted in the hollow, but from a hundred yards away the mountains only make it a bigger outhouse. Nowadays he's senile and his clothesline is always lined with his underwear. If they were clean I know a few people who might consider stealing a pair because Ernie Skiles' place is soon to follow and it's wise to cover one's nose. People say it's the sows his father keeps, but I'm sure there is more to that smell hanging over his property than mud and pigs.

I won't see our two-block town, complete with a Go-Mart, Mr. Dollar, auto body shop, unisex hair salon, and two churches, until the last curve after Corey's Gas. There are also a couple of drinking holes, but they're tucked away from what some people call the "business district" in order to make the place "more respectable"—although I can't say anyone comes to walk around, take in the atmosphere, or to feel proud about the place.

I reach town and walk towards Four Seasons Showcase, a turn of the century, two-story, red brick building. I've always expected the place to get more attention since it's not a name-brand chain or the kind of shop normally found in a tiny community like Deerfoil. It's owned by Mr. Shearer, an Englishman who bought the building several years ago and lives upstairs while running an art gallery on the first floor, mostly of his own paintings and drawings. His studio is in the back of the building where he paints almost daily if he's not out of town. Most people in the area have forgotten Four Seasons exists, or at least they act that way. Its oddity can't crack the popularity of drinking—or the churches, the hair fixing, engines, and candy bars.

Mr. Shearer's work reveals the land, the sky, and the different colors that shine down on us throughout the day. I think he is searching for a beauty that people here find strange. The people in his artwork appear unclear and out of focus, as if life goes on in one big haze. I've seen more than a few people laugh at those paintings and heard them say Mr. Shearer is a nut, that if this is what people are like in England, they don't want any part of it.

Mr. Shearer moved here from Alexandria, Virginia, just to open his gallery. I believe he was a lawyer there for many years, but he says that's one part of his life that's not worth talking about. I know people who breed dogs, run meth labs, sell cosmetics, or start any number of failed businesses here, but the difference is that Mr. Shearer doesn't mind if he sells a single painting all year. No one buys paintings from his gallery, but he doesn't change anything. A few people suggested that he sell trinkets, ceramics, and Hallmark cards, but he says profits are not the point.

This week Mr. Shearer went to Washington, D.C. for an art show, so I figure that helps him accept that no one here is very interested. He goes to shows once every two or three months and says he's happy to take me if I have permission. I guess that's part of our working relationship, for lack of a better term. When he's out of town or busy, I open his shop and look after it for him. I clean or help him move things, do whatever he needs done. In exchange, I get free painting lessons and a place to hang out where we chat, drink tea, and play chess. On Sundays the gallery is always closed, but I go there anyway.

Unlocking the door, I move quickly inside to turn off the security alarm. Then I lock back up and walk to the rear where I turn on a light and go into the studio. My eyes go to the thirty-by-thirty canvas I'm working on with Mr. Shearer. It's almost halfway finished. It's an image of a road in the mountains, but the road doesn't really go anywhere—only an exercise in perspective.

Whenever I enter the studio, it's never long before my attention turns to Mr. Shearer's paintings, all at different levels of completion. Some are barely touched while others appear finished. Maybe he'll keep adding small details or maybe he just wants some time to pass to see if he's content with what he's painted. Some works he paints over altogether.

About six months ago he painted one of a man on the street corner at dusk. Unidentifiable stores stand forlornly behind him. Pristine mountains stretch above, and with the way Mr. Shearer can do it, the mountains somehow appear both protective and threatening. The man in the painting is tall and probably young by the looks of his upright posture and full head of light-brown hair. He holds a lit cigarette and wears working-class clothing: soiled boots, old jeans, and a worn flannel shirt—but the face is ghost-like with no emotions or any real features. That's the part that makes me look back at it over and over again as if it owns me.

Looking at it now, I think about the morning service starting. Pops will testify, speak about Mom, and some will go down to the altar to pray for her. I figure I should say a prayer here too. I hope they can get it all out of her. I hope she doesn't die. I don't want another funeral. I don't want more talk about hellfire. Their funeral stares are like more tumors. Maybe all of it is payback for our spitting on each other and the land so much. That beautiful land Mr. Shearer always paints so well is the inspiration that brought him here, he says.

I move to my easel and squeeze some Prussian blue paint onto my palette, mix it with a glaze. I pick up a small brush and load it with paint. I look back again at the man on the street corner in Mr. Shearer's painting, then start on the canvas. If I can learn something about perspective, I might be able to paint the mountains and hollows and faces in my own way, open up my own stories that I have no other way to tell.

Sleepwalkers

They were keepsakes, those moments when he entered my room. I carried them around in my chest, in my pockets, to school, like other kids carried coins or candy or Matchbox cars.

I'd listen for the arrival of his Mazda he'd park just off the driveway. Or the creak of the basement door as he came up from his bedroom. I'd listen for his forceful stride coming down the hallway, then hide the comics, hide whatever he'd disapprove or laugh about as immature.

There is no picture frame to display this captain. That thrill—the hope of an invitation to search the attic, drive for groceries, anything—could never be hung on the wall.

Come here, brother. Come again. Come for your own mission, but come. Come down that narrow corridor of hard walls, my bedroom at the end of the hallway.

He'd mostly enter pissed: frustrated with Mom and Dad, work, society. Now it was his time to let out the backwash, the fire and brimstone, pent-up. That's what I didn't want, Captain. Air, fresh air, always so hard to come by; mine suffocating, too, in a windowless, closed-door room: stale, without circulation.

But you were right, Captain. They stab at us while wearing body armor, throw out hooks loaded with all sorts of bait. Something wears away, something in us gets filed down to nubs. And they look at our faces, try to fix us with a stare, remove what they don't like. Now I understand they were watching you, too, before you disappeared.

I lean. I rise. I stand up in the darkness. The day is done and we have turned off life. It's a soft sound, soft touch, when the

103

balls of my feet reach down to the throw rug. We live here, eat off this ground. But where is our soil?

No tap. No click. No rubber soles. But with measured steps I am moving again. Only the bottom of my bare feet rubs the treated wood, the room itself fearful of calling out, quietly counting the blinks of my eyes. I cannot say what I see, cannot say how the door opens each time, the wind in my hands, how a little tug lifts the latch without a click, why the hammer does not explode from its hollow space.

I reach the soft warmth of the plush carpet outside my room, dust and the spider surprised by their error in the forecast. I don›t know if my worry is suspended at that time: the fear of making a noise, knocking over mother's ceramics, turning on a light that ruins their darkness. I don't know if there are colors in the pitch black, or depth to the hallway. I don't know if there are grooves and crevices in the wall, or pain if my knee bangs into it. I can't say if communication has no offer, preferences are dry, or the chest is loaded with thoughts. I only know it's certainly better to make it back alone, my tricky moment of history unrecorded, a phantom to their assessment. If I succeed and lie back down undetected, there are no flowers, no eulogy.

The first time they caught me was the night he threw down his half-eaten plum and walked away from our hotel room at Nag's Head, angry that Dad yelled at him for not folding his clothes. A policeman brought him back two days later and he wouldn't say a word to me, wouldn't speak to any of us for the remainder of summer vacation. There was no space for me to roam that night, and since then it's gotten even harder. Now they watch, hawk-veined, listening for the pitter-patter.

"What are you doing, man?" he finally asked me a few years later. He had just arrived home from work and had an unopened Pretenders album under his arm. "How can you walk like that in the dark?"

I felt lost to him as well sometimes. Instead of answering his question, I wanted to ask if he would help me rake the leaves the next day. Those reds, oranges, and yellows making beautiful fire on the ground. I hated wiping them up for father, scraping the soil with those screechy, metal fingers of his burdening tools.

"Go to sleep and stay asleep," my Captain said in his condescending way that Friday night. Then he left again, to Willy's or Night Owl or The Den. He wouldn't stay with me very long. There was too much pushing him to the outside, and wheels make us believe we can go anywhere.

It was the same every weekend. I wouldn't see him again until Sunday after morning church services. Then my Captain and I would go for Sunday lunch at grandmother's house.

"Hurry up," he always said.

I'd always eat very little, but I wanted to go anyway. Grandma would put the food in front of us with the duty of another generation, and sometimes I thought about grandfather who never left a seed or a speck or a stain on his plate.

Captain would eat piles of food. If his mind was rested, he would tell me a funny story as he ate. Otherwise there was silence except for the dinner commands. "Give me those green beans." "Any sweet potatoes left?" I wondered how and why he ate so much. Mostly I sat waiting to serve his commands, eating little until Grandmother gave me comforting nudges.

Sometimes I got dreamy over the sweet tea and looked up the hill behind the house where grandfather grew his corn, half runners, and spring onions. I never got a chance to see where those mountains led, never figured out why some things are unspoken, but I believed that high up on the ridge there were creatures no one had seen, creatures feeding on something different, creatures that maybe people used to care about.

Mother is on the phone when I get home from school, "worried sick." Talking to Brenda or Nancy or Kathy. I hear her talking about me just like she talked about him, telling people who are more interested in their own pleasure than genuine concern. I feel a crawling emptiness when she gives up my secrets. I would rather she talked to the trees like the lunatic at the end of the road, for the more she tells them the more strange stares I receive. "I don't know what we're going to do."

I'll get both ends of the conversation when Dad arrives. "This is troubling." "He's going overboard." "He's too old for this." "His priorities are all wrong." For sure. Just like my Captain used to hear, but they squandered any chance to reach him and the rope they fastened around him went to the wrong spot.

I always thought, why not get your own boat, Captain? Forget the cargo lost on this one. Seven generations were jumped between grandmother and us, and the gap is too great, caves in on itself, our minds.

Little Nikki keeps playing. She's easy and walks over into Grandmother's arms.

But what does she see when she's seated in the chair? She's brought in a blue jay feather this afternoon. Earlier it was a six-inch-tall mushroom, a robin's egg, and a mole's skull.

"Why do you bring in these dirty things?" Mother always asks.

But I think how Nikki will outlive us both, Captain and I. Not just because she's younger, but because she believes in putting her hands in the dirt. Hand slaps are not changing her. She rolls pebbles on the church pew and puts milkweed plants in hymnals.

When Grandmother is babysitting she sees it too, even pokes and prods to help it seep out. "Bring me some moss, a pinecone, and elderberries," she says.

Nikki wanders out the back door and into the woods. Mother is not there to disapprove or assign plastic games.

"Now bury that coin under the moss," Grandmother says. "And go back for some twigs so we can make a forest."

When Mother arrives, she will complain of the smell, the soil. Grandmother will snicker when Nikki tells Mom that the earth is a safe place.

He came to me one day. "You know why you've been doing this for so long?" I didn't answer. "Because you're a lot like me. It's anxiety, from being lost in their rubble." I smiled. "I lash, I fight, I throw it out, but you just keep it in. So where's it going to go? And when? That's it! It tries to let itself out at night when you aren't in control anymore."

I nodded when he asked if I knew what he meant. He said my name and shook his head.

My Captain worried about me, but I didn't know why. I only knew there were grand spaces that I didn't understand, an empty theater, mysterious caves. My Captain wanted to find them, reside there, but he never succeeded.

And me? I keep rising from the bed, sometimes going downstairs to sit on the ground in the basement, trying to smell him. Stairs are never an obstacle. Furniture no obstacle. Darkness means nothing. Maybe my Captain was right. Maybe what is inside of me wants released, tired of living without a name.

Yes, front doors, back doors, no matter the locks, all open during the night. How far does the path go? I wish I could ask Captain, but he'd have no answers either. The highways are a mirage and what is poured inside us is difficult to drain. We want to turn back at the door, but there isn't enough inside us.

A few months ago they heard me at the front door. When I turned back, Father stood in the hallway in his holey underwear. Under his arm he steadied the unloaded rifle stored in his bedroom closet, pointed it at me.

I heard them talking in the doctor's office.

"He's been sleepwalking off and on for a few years now, but it's gotten noticeably worse the last six months."

"Any signs of depression, anxiety, or anti-social behavior?"

"No, not really. He's a quiet kid, good student."

"Any medications, seizures, or sleep deprivation?"

"No."

"Any other issues or irregularities?"

"No, not really."

"Probably not much to worry about then. Just be practical. Put away any dangerous items that he could get a hold of. Lock the doors and windows. Anything that would reduce the risk of an accident. Otherwise, make sure he's getting enough sleep and he should grow out of it."

"We're just worried he'll turn out like our older son."

I woke to hear Father tell him, "You're better than that, son." Captain didn't reply. Mother's faint weeping started and didn't stop. A few more sentences and then, "We taught you better than that." Father talked slowly, what might sound relaxed to an outsider, but I knew it meant he was resigned for once.

They say I found him two weeks later when I went downstairs to sit outside his room again. They say his door was open and he was hanging in the closet, but I have no recollection. If I saw him, it was in some other world.

Father followed me down, but I had already turned to walk up the stairs when he began yelling my brother's name.

They asked me what I saw over and over again. I could not give them an answer. I could say nothing. I was no better than that.

Now he is in their yard of stones. I wonder if I could have taught him how it's done, convinced him to walk with me during the night. Maybe then he could still visit me on occasion.

I know the doctor wasn't right. I have not grown out of it. My Captain was correct. "It's anxiety, from being lost in their rubble."

"We're really worried about him," I heard Mom say again on the telephone last week. "I think it's twice as bad as it was last year."

Some nights I still walk downstairs. Last month, Dad found me in my Captain's closet, standing with my head tilted. So yesterday they told me I have to start taking Desyrel.

The picture frames never existed, but now they have ruined even the pictures. I'd like to leave my room some night and walk straight through the mirror still hanging on the wall of my Captain's bedroom. I'd like to see him again. Lie down and finally rest together.

POSTCARDS

"*Que fea!*" a teenage girl blurted out from across the room, breaking Johnny's concentration as he stared at an upright fetus seated behind glass, the world's smallest mummy in a museum dedicated to mummies. The word *momia* sounded like mommy, reminding him he hadn't sent his mother a postcard in a couple of days.

"*Y que piensas?*" his fiancée asked, rushing up to his side in her jeans skirt and pink blouse.

"*Que* what?" Johnny replied.

"What do you think about it?" Lupita translated.

"Interesting, I guess."

Lupita had asked him his opinion of the mummy, but she may as well have asked what he thought of all Mexico. After three tiring days of bus travel from Charleston, they'd arrived a week ago in her hometown. Mother always said she was a good speller, but damned if she could spell Guanajuato. Lupita's family had welcomed him with delicious food—*chiles en Nogada, sopa Azteca,* and *flan de coco* just last night—dispelling all the intestinal nightmares that people back home had warned him about. Still, so much was blurry as he sought to adjust. From Spanish to extended family life, the week seemed like a series of wild flashes that he couldn't get a hold of—indistinguishable shapes and strange noises. To compensate, his mind often wandered back home, especially to his mother.

Johnny moved on to the next mummy display. Some of the faces reminded him of cartoon characters. How could a mummy look like Patrick Star? A few of the faces appeared genuinely jolly despite many dying during the 1833 cholera outbreak. A small number of them were even buried alive as officials rushed to cover the bodies and prevent the spread of disease. Some of the mummies showed fear in their faces though, like the man whose head tilted back, mouth agape as if screaming. Further down, his legs spread wide open to reveal a bare pelvis and stick-like limbs with old, faded work boots tied on to the end of the stumps.

Peasant clothes covered another mummy, its thinned, grey hair and crooked teeth reminding Johnny of Teddy, his alcoholic uncle. Johnny had tried to get him hired at Tres Salsas where he himself met Lupita while working as a waiter. Johnny could still see out the large window by the booths where he had taken so many orders in Montgomery. The sidewalks in front of the restaurant had been under construction for over a year, but even after the new concrete was laid crowds never appeared.

Across the street the admissions building to the state university maintained the only real business in the small town. People knew the few remaining businesses wouldn't survive if the school ever closed. The town's buildings and retirees would slowly die, watching even more of the youth and working-aged leave. Tres Salsas would have the same fate since the older generation rarely ate the chimichangas, enchiladas, and burritos that Johnny now realized were not genuine Mexican food.

"I'll bring you some deer meat next weekend," he recalled Obert repeating to the new waiter who had recently arrived from Guadalajara and spoke only basic English. Johnny felt awkward for Jose. What the hell did this kid from Guadalajara want to hear about deer meat that was nothing more than the dead flesh of Obert's ego? Jose didn't even know the word deer in English.

Obert was just clueless to language and cultural differences, but Johnny's father spouted aggression. "Mexico?" he yelled when Johnny mentioned his idea one evening to get engaged with Lupita and move back home with her to Guanajuato. "Them Mexicans are nothing but Indians. They'll scalp a wimp like you in under a week, son."

"Honey," Mother said emptily, trying to blow her feather of intervention into the air, always the polite rabbit up against an archaic beast.

"Of all the crazy things a man'll do while chasing a woman," his father continued. "You think you're going to clean toilets down there for twenty dollars an hour?" he asked, shaking his head. "This beats all I've ever heard. Cincinnati, Lexington, Charlotte, your crazy uncle even went to Atlanta. But Mexico? Aren't even any white hips that good. Peggy, I told you that son had a screw loose."

Although a full year passed before Lupita returned home and Johnny followed her, his father's venom only convinced Johnny he should go. He wanted a place with stronger traditions, deeper family roots, and a more vibrant culture than his own. He wanted to get away from his own father. He loved Lupita as well and hoped one day when they had children that her strong, straight nose would remedy the pug snouts traveling through his own lineage.

Even when he told his plan to a few people he trusted, all the reactions were negative. Danny said he better get used to living with diarrhea if he was heading south of the border, and Rusty told him he'd call up the Pope to see if he'd expedite his passport. Others told him it would be better just to go to Cincinnati or somewhere closer so that he could come back home after a couple of years.

"That's how they are," Johnny whispered to himself while staring into the eye sockets of another mummy. He reminded himself again to buy his mother another postcard before leaving the museum, preferably not of mummies.

Lupita came over and put her arm around Johnny's waist, made him feel good. He liked her way of making him feel comfortable, so different from his earlier girlfriends.

"You're quiet," she said.

"Yeah, just kind of interested in all this," he replied with a half-truth.

"I'm happy, Johnny," Lupita said, snuggling up closer. "I still can't believe you came here just for me."

Johnny smiled. "How many more rooms are there in the museum?"

"Only two more," she answered, squeezing him tighter.

It took only a few minutes to walk through the remaining two rooms. Johnny looked at each display without stopping. Thinking of home and his mother had ended most of his interest in the mummies.

"Are you excited about the welcome party tonight?" Lupita asked when he turned from the last display. Her family had organized yet another event to embrace the arrival of their future son-in-law. Many of Lupita's extended family had already stopped by the house to meet him, but the welcome party would be a more official gathering for the entire family and neighborhood.

"Sure. It's real kind of them," Johnny replied, genuinely impressed with the family's hospitality. "Sorry my family never did the same thing for you." Lupita didn't reply. "Listen, before we leave, can we go back to pick up another postcard for Mom?"

"You want to send her a picture of a *momia*?" Lupita asked as she steered him back toward the lobby.

"No, no, maybe something else. We can see which postcards they've got. Seeing these dried-up faces wouldn't help Mom feel any better about my leaving."

In the gift shop Johnny saw the museum's collection of postcards near the ticket counter. They walked up to the rotating display holders, filled with pictures of mummies in the museum as expected. Lupita quickly suggested a cartoon drawing of a mummy in a suit. Johnny refused it and Lupita turned the holder to another column of preserved cadavers.

On the last stand they found a picture of three frogs and the main cathedral of the town. Lupita explained that Guanajuato meant "The Hill of Frogs" in P'urhepecha, and that it was also a nickname of people from the state.

"Well, maybe Mom will remember the time I caught a few frogs in the creek and tried to keep them as pets," Johnny said as he wondered what meaning his mother would attach to the pictures.

"Johnny, we can go back into the center of town tomorrow where there's a better selection if you don't want to send this one," Lupita offered.

"Yeah, I know, but I kind of wanted to write Mom tonight."

"Well, why don't you write her a letter on paper and just send that instead? That way you can write more than you can fit on a tiny postcard."

"Nah. Mom said to send her postcards. She likes looking at the pictures."

"Even if it's just cartoon frogs?"

"Yeah, she likes to put them up on her refrigerator using these magnets that are all different fruits. Remember I already sent two others since we left, so this isn't the only postcard she'll be getting."

"Hope this one doesn't arrive first," Lupita said, giggling. Johnny did not hear her, however, as he dug into his pocket for a few coins and walked to the counter with the postcard in hand. "Yeah, she'll be happy to see them up on the refrigerator, frogs and all."

Amelda loved them. If she read one, she had to read them all. The postcards gave her smiles, pride, and memories, the best she had, but if she could see him at home again, she'd gladly throw them all away or stuff them in a shoebox.

> *Dear Mom,*   *April 11, 2008*
> *Well, we finally made it to Houston. Seems like it's a week later but I guess it's only a day and a half. Lupe slept on the bus, but I couldn't. Houston's a big, big city, and Texas feels like a foreign country to me almost. Atlanta was big too, but it was dark when we got in and changed buses. Had a big burger and sleeping at Days Inn. Tomorrow it's another bus to M-E-X-I-C-O! People said I couldn't do it, but I'm almost there. Hope you're feeling okay.*
> *Love you, Johnny*

> *Dear Mom,*   *April 13, 2008*
> *You know I won't miss everything about home, but you still feel homesick just almost immediately after crossing the border into Mexico. Strange. Everything changes instantly. Everything. Even the dirt. Even the smell. Even Mexican food. Another long bus ride to get to Mexico City and we changed buses to go to Lupe's hometown. We went to her parents' house where they gave me a small room of my own. I don't know what to write about there is so much. Right now just trying to get used to it all. I'll write more when I do. So I'm here!!!*
> *Johnny*

She moved on to her favorite, the one that made her laugh every time.

> *Dear Mom,*   *April 16, 2008*
> *Sorry about the frogs—hope this one doesn't arrive first! The name of Lupe's city means hill of frogs in one of the languages here. Best I can do since we're*

at a mummy museum today. Yes, a mummy museum, not mommy museum. All the other postcards were pictures of mummies. Kind of cool, but I didn't want a mummy sleeping on your refrigerator. I'm getting ready now for the welcome party her family is giving me tonight. Nervous since it will be more than 100 people and I doubt anyone speaks English but Lupe. Now I know 50 words in Spanish, but I can't spend the whole evening saying, "How much?" and "Where is the bathroom?" I'll be too busy stuffing myself anyway because it'll be a feast.

Love, Johnny

Johnny's mother removed her glasses and set them down on the table beside the small pile of postcards and a can of mixed nuts. Through the window the sky darkened as a wren finished its song and prepared to roost under the eave above the porch. She pushed her chair back slowly and stood up, grimacing because of her bruised ribs. From the refrigerator she took out a two liter of Coca-Cola, then picked up a glass on the table and began to pour. The black liquid rushed to the top of the glass with a thick layer of fizz and foam.

A door burst open causing the plates and glasses on the shelves to shake. A bulky man hooked on alcohol wobbled inside, frightening her as usual. She knew he was drunk again, probably had been drinking since he left in the morning. Amelda had plenty of evidence to justify her fear, and she put the bottle of soda aside to give her husband the same consideration she'd give a black bear in the woods. Even from across the living room she could see Jim's bloodshot eyes shining red in the void of the door he left open behind him. She hoped he would go straight upstairs and fall asleep, but he stopped and stared at her in a disoriented gaze.

"A pile of postcards," he said, his tongue almost a barrier to communication. "That's all you've got from spending twenty years to raise that boy." She stood and listened, head down, knowing it unwise to move or speak. "Just a pile of stupid papers that you treat like gold. You take pride in that, old woman?"

He moved to the kitchen and she sat back down in her chair to avoid him, gathering the postcards and putting them behind the toaster. He opened the refrigerator door, his large hand moving items around inside. She knew he was looking for a beer.

"You drank the last beer yesterday evening, dear."

He didn't hear her as he shuffled a few more bottles and containers around before accepting defeat. His head lifted from inside the refrigerator, a shadowy block of darkness against the light, and he closed the door. She could hear his breathing intensify in disgust. His glare turned to the table, and his open hand flew forward, slapping her across the cheek. The follow-through knocked over her glass and the Coca-Cola spread over the wooden table, fizzing again.

"Twenty-five-cent postcards is enough to make you happy? Guess they don't have no telephones down there in all that filth. What kind of son goes to a shit hole like that?"

When she looked up again he had gone. The stairs creaked above her. She stood up, went to the kitchen counter for a dry rag, and began to clean the sticky soda off of the table, relieved that the postcards were saved.

She refilled her glass of Coca-Cola, placed an almond in her mouth, and sat back down to pick up where she had left off.

> *Hola! (Hello),*   *April 19, 2008*
> *I don't think I'll ever enjoy Taco Bell again! I know you won't believe me, but it's true!!! I love the food here and I love Lupe! I'm starting to know the town and I finally took out my Spanish book. Mrs. Perry would be shocked! At first the town kind of scared me, but now I'm getting used to it. There is an underground road that leads into the town so that traffic won't be so crowded. Lupe's family is treating me great. Better than Dad would ever treat Lupe, that's for sure. But never mind that. One day you'll come visit.*
>
>   *Johnny*

She bit her lip when she came to the sentence about his father, the man she met when Johnny was already two months in her womb.

> *Dear Mom,*   *April 27, 2008*
> *Sorry I haven't written for a week. No problems, just getting used to the new life here. I wish you could taste some of the fruits. I ate a pineapple yesterday that was*

*so fresh and tangy that it burned my lips! All kinds
of new drinks too that the people make fresh. People
are treating me real nice and I don't have any problems
really. Lupe says hello. I think I'm going to start taking
a Spanish class in town. Trying to learn this stuff on
my own just doesn't cut it and it's embarrassing not
understanding what people say to you when there is a
smile on their face. I miss you, Mom, but things are
going great here. Don't worry!*

Love, Johnny

The thought of Johnny starting a new life lifted her spirits.
Her eyes watered. If he needed to go to a foreign country to find
some peace, so be it.

Hi Mom,   May 6, 2008
*Just got back from a trip to the country today and got
your letter! Thanks! Lupe took me to an old hacienda,
this old estate. We ate a great meal and had a nice walk
around. Very relaxing. The air was so fresh and clean.
Great weather! I don't know why people talk about dir-
tiness and diarrhea when anyone mentions Mexico. Most
places actually seem cleaner than at home. I had my
first Spanish class last week and it was kind of fun
actually. I met a few other Americans there. Adrian
from Florida, an older man from Santa Barbara, and a
couple from Indiana who are missionaries. They asked
me if I was one too. I told them that I was a missionary
for love, but they didn't get my joke and thought I really
was a missionary!*

Love, Johnny

She wasn't sure if she got the joke either, but Johnny's
passion came through his short messages. In youth there are fewer
limits and worries, more hope and passion, she thought, but it
passes quickly. As with her own life, the shine of Johnny's would
one day start to fall, slowly at first, then with increasing speed.
She turned on the small table lamp and stood up to turn off the
kitchen lights, letting the rest of the first floor fall to darkness. Each
postcard now moved her beyond Johnny's details and towards a

contemplation of her own dreams and life. She thought of the retirement house in Florida Jim had once promised her. Now she would settle for a one-week vacation there and a chance to send a postcard of her own. The light on the table grew stronger and the rest of the room and world seemed to fall away, hiding the twisted creatures that loomed as shadows on the walls.

She tried to settle her mind after reading Johnny's most recent postcard. It had arrived last week on the final day of August. She put the postcards back on the refrigerator, meticulously arranged, and cleaned off the table. She turned off the table lamp and stood in the darkness. The illumination of a streetlight fought to get inside the house as she readied herself to go upstairs.

Johnny put his pen down and read what he had written.

> *Dear Mom,*   *January 8, 2009*
> *How are you? I miss you. Just wanted to let you know that Lupe and I moved into our own apartment just like we were hoping to do. Work is going well also. I'd ask you to come down, but I know it's better you don't because we don't want any problems with Dad. Maybe later this year Lupe and I can visit when I get a couple weeks off from work. How is the weather there? Any snow yet? Of course, down here I don't even know what cold weather is. Wouldn't mind some cold weather actually, although I'm sure that sounds kind of crazy to you. Okay, it's time for dinner. Don't get jealous from the picture, I'm 500 miles away from Acapulco.*

He turned to the window. Chilly, grey sleet covered the streets. He looked at his own cold hand and wondered again if the landlord would ever turn up the heat, a problem he never had to worry about in Mexico. He stood up to pour some more coffee, the headache at his temples telling him not to go to work. He wished he could go back to sleep in his new bed, wished it was like school when they called the whole day off due to bad road conditions.

Another sip of coffee and he went back to the postcard. He had forgotten to sign it. He quickly wrote his name and then took out the Mexican stamps he had brought back with him, sticking

117

two on the corner as usual. He wondered how long he could maintain the deception; this was the third postcard he had written since arriving back in Charleston. Sooner or later his mother would wonder why he was not answering a question she had sent to him, or he would run out of the postcards and stamps from Mexico, or the kid at work he paid to deliver the postcards to his mother's mailbox would be seen. It was unlikely, but the worst would be running into her at work.

Outside, the fog hovered and kept its own pace, unaffected by the cars that knifed through. Johnny finished his coffee and put on his shoes. He switched off the lights and opened the door, stepped out on to the icy steps, postcard in hand. Maybe today he would even make a phone call to his mother, a phone call from Guanajuato.

The Handyman's Heat

Dick Kumil eases his royal blue Sunfire up to the mailbox and stretches his tubby torso across the front seat to roll down the passenger window. "Going to church anywhere these days, son?"

I step toward the car and smell his musty body odor shooting from the vehicle. Even Dick's own son won't sit next to him; Danny's four years younger than me and gives a nod from the back seat as he fiddles with a fluorescent fishing lure, his mouth hanging open as usual. When I last saw Dick a few days ago, he was pitching another losing game of horseshoes with a tall can of Schlitz in his free hand, the curse words tumbling out of his mouth when he wasn't tipping the golden liquid back. I pay little attention to him, but his property sits next to Josh Staples' basketball-rimmed driveway, and it's almost always the same scene when I wander over to shoot some hoops.

"Nah. Just getting ready to go back to school tomorrow," I reply, Frisbee in hand. How low will Mom go to get me back into church?

Dick twists his neck so he can get his head parallel with the dashboard and make some sort of screwed up eye contact. "College ain't nothing if you ain't saved," he says. He's got his shirt off any day it hits seventy degrees, so no surprise his belly flab is resting on the bottom of the steering wheel in an August scorcher, gleaming in sweat despite the rumbling air conditioner. Honey oil, he calls it.

"Understood, Dick."

"I know your folks taught you right."

"Yeah."

"My wife saw your mother out at Kroger the other day. What are you studying at Marshall anyway?"

"WVU."

"All right. What are you studying in Morganhole then?" His face shrivels from the neck craning. Danny's looking out the window at the Freeman's bulldog barking in their yard.

"Don't know yet. Might major in history. I'm in a liberal arts program."

"That's what I figured. Them liberal schools nowadays do their best to brainwash you pups. Better make sure you study something you can put to use for the Lord."

Dick sits back up in his seat and takes off his Amoco hat. He scratches his head and wipes his brow. An open container of dry roasted peanuts lies on its side in the seat next to him, and he angles his fingers into it to pull out a few. For a moment I fear he might cut the motor.

"Well, it's Friday. I'll be seeing you later down my way I suppose," he calls across the seat as he chews. "You be sure and think about what I've said."

In the evening Mom prepares a big dinner since I'm leaving the next morning: a Hormel ham, half runners from the farmer's market, cornbread, cucumbers and spring onions from the garden.

"Heck, you can't beat this Matt," Dad says, once we all get seated at the kitchen table. "Smell that cornbread fresh out of the oven. Your tacos and rice can't touch this." He wants another food argument that always ends with "If it ain't broke, don't fix it."

"Guess who drove by the house this afternoon, Mom?" I ask, lifting a glass of iced tea filled to the rim after I added two more ice cubes.

"I don't know, Matthew. Wade Boggs? Cecil Fielder? Freddie Prince?"

"Dick Kumil."

"Dick Kumil? I don't believe I know a Dick Kumil," Mom says as she spoons vinegar from the bowl of onions and cucumbers onto her green beans.

"You don't know a Dick Kumil? The guy who fixes our air conditioner, dishwasher, all the gadgets."

"Ohhh. You mean Dick."

"Yes, I mean Dick Kumil. The handyman who doesn't wear a handy belt and shows you his hairy ass-crack every time he bends over."

"Matthew."

"Then don't act like you've never heard of him."

"Does he really, Laura?" Dad asks.

"Tom, I haven't seen him in months. Pass me the cornbread, please."

"Whatever, Mom. He stopped by the house today just to ask if I've been going to church. And Dick never drives up here unless he's got a job."

"So what's wrong with asking you that? He's right. You ought to be going."

"You know as well as I do that Dick cares about church as much as you care about Judas Priest."

"What?"

"Mom, just stop having people pressure me into church all the time. Last month, Bud Bench offered to get me clothing discounts at American Eagle if I went to Vacation Bible School, and three weeks ago Mary Belcher told me I could sit with her daughter during Sunday night services. Now it's Dick Kumil, and he's offering nothing but body odor and a bloated belly."

"You exaggerate, Matthew. But I guess you don't realize how embarrassing it is when the other women in the choir ask me how you're doing and why you're not in church. I can't even fix a pan of brownies for bake sales anymore without your old Sunday school teacher Loretta Flowers asking me when you're coming to church. And by the way, maybe Dick turned his heart over to the Lord. That's not so crazy."

I shake my head and swallow a bite of cornbread. "Sure he has. And I hope he goes to the Mountain Chapel without a belt on Sunday mornings, too. Then you all can take that to the Lord in prayer."

"Matthew, you were never this cocky before. Or filthy. Is this what they taught you during your freshman year at college?"

"That and atheism and communism," Dad chimes in, barely understandable with the slice of ham in his mouth.

The next morning Gerald Salisbury stops by the house to pick me up. His parents gave him a little Honda Civic when we graduated from Calvin Coolidge, so I pay for the gas and he drives us to Morgantown each semester. The arrangement is completely a practical one because Gerry and I have little in common. I like basketball and skateboarding and he likes shopping malls. I'm interested in impressionism and he's interested in supply-side economics. Mom likes him because he sings in his church choir. That means we have little to talk about on the four-hour ride back to the university, five hours counting the stop at Tudor's. But this time, instead of waiting for me in the car, he rings the doorbell and Mom invites him inside the house.

In the kitchen, Mom gives Gerry breakfast and then stocks a "treat basket" for him that includes fresh pears, a tin of chocolate chip cookies she baked, and blueberry licorice from her trip to Amish country in Ohio. She even adds an evergreen air freshener to "Gerry's bag." Despite the smell of bacon, I'm in a daze since it's the first morning in weeks that I've gotten up before ten o'clock. I don't think much about Mom's kindness except to figure it's her usual friendly self.

Gerry polishes off the scrambled eggs, toast with grape jelly, and Bob Evans bacon, and I say my goodbyes. Dad and I carry my luggage out of the house and stuff it in the tiny car. Ten minutes later Gerry and I are cruising up I-79, and he starts talking about Fairleigh Baptist's summer singing tour. The usually quiet drive turns into his non-stop talk about church. I stare out the window at the green hills lit up by the sun as I short-answer his questions—mostly rhetorical ones anyway. But after twenty minutes he's still going on about brotherhood and fellowship. I try to change the subject, fake a nap, turn on the radio to a light rock station, but nothing slows Gerry down. The interstate twists and turns through the mountains while his mouth jabbers away like we're on a straight stretch.

"You know, you're starting to remind me of Dick Kumil," I finally say. "And I know it's on my mom's behalf just to get me to go to church. I've heard her telling my dad she wants me back in services."

"Who's Dick Kumil?" he asks, ignoring the more important point.

"He's a middle-aged, fix-it man who lives in my neighborhood, a total sinner. A couple days ago, out of the blue, he drove past our house and stopped to talk to me about church, telling me I should be going, giving me the guilt-trip and all. I'm sure Mom put him up to it."

Gerry passes a white Ford truck spitting out grey exhaust

as we climb a hill. "Why think it's your mom, Matt? There are lots of people who like to talk about church."

"Gerry, I've known Dick Kumil since I was eight years old. That's more than ten years ago, and other than fixing an appliance or two I've never seen him do anything but drink Schlitz and paint his backyard with curse words. The only advice he ever gave me was to grab a beer and not take my studies too seriously. He's never even had a regular job either—other than going to Beer Exchange to pick up more Schlitz. And if he's ever cleaned anything on occasion, it'd be his own ass. I'm not even sure that gets a regular washing."

Gerry turns the air conditioner down a notch as he holds back his laughter. "Does he have a family?"

"Yeah. Three sons and his wife. And you should ask my friend Josh about it. Josh's sister is only thirteen and he says that Dick Kumil undresses her with his eyes every time he sees her."

"That's not good. So how's he support his family if he just does small jobs here and there?"

"His wife Candy is a nurse at CAMC."

"Candy Kumil?"

"Yeah. And as far as I know, she takes care of the house as well. She even cuts the lawn. Like I said, other than making an occasional housecall to fix something, all I've ever seen Dick do is drink, talk, and sling horseshoes."

"Come on, Matt."

"I'm serious. I remember one day in 10th grade when I was walking home from school. He stood at the edge of his driveway collecting mail and stopped me to ask what book I was carrying. I handed it to him and he goes, 'Hope you're enjoying your Mr. Flowbert. That Madame Ovary was a fine book writer.'"

"Well, maybe he's changed. And anyway, you don't have to know your fairy tales to be a Christian."

I sigh. "Gerry, pull off the next exit. I need a toilet bad."

"How are classes, Matthew?" Mom asks me two weeks later when I make the semester's first bimonthly call home as requested, Gerald Salisbury and Dick Kumil forgotten.

"Fine, Mom," I answer, ripping the nail off my big toe while hoping she can't hear my dormmates cursing outside my room. "I like all of them so far except for my calculus class."

"What's wrong with calculus?"

"I'm just tired of math, and Professor Hamad has the personality of a turtle. In monotone."

"Well, make sure you work just as hard in calculus as the other classes."

"I will."

"How's the weather up there? Make any new friends?"

"Yeah, sure, but Gerry's in a dorm on the other side of campus and I haven't seen him since he dropped me off, if that's what you're asking. You two got along so well." I rip another toenail off and a little blood flows out of the quick.

"No, no. I wasn't referring to him."

"I guess you know he talked about church for most of our drive up to school."

"No. How would I know that?"

"Just like you had Dick Kumil drive by."

"Oh my, Matthew. You're still paranoid about that? And for your information, Dick got saved about six months ago. In fact, I just saw Candy at Foodland last week, and she says he's been called to preach. The Lord spoke to him one evening. In the bathtub."

When I get home for winter break, Dick Kumil's horseshoe poles no longer stand, and the large recycling bucket of beer cans that always sat on his back porch is gone. A white flag that reads "Jesus Saves" in bright green letters has replaced a Bud Light poster in the window next to his front door, and numerous "God First" stickers cover the mailbox which once showed a cardinal perched on the edge of a wintry forest. He won't even let Candy put up a Christmas tree on account that it's pagan.

I visit Josh's house a few times over the break, mostly to play video games. On one occasion Dick's at his mailbox blowing into his hands as if he's stood in the cold for hours. "Guess Josh and me won't have any reason this summer to come over anymore, Dick. No horseshoes. No lawn parties."

"Oh, you fellows can come over anytime, son. Don't you worry about that. We'll play Bible bingo and you can drink all the Country Time you want. We'll have the good stuff. Including church people."

On a rainy morning at the end of June, Mom says to me, "Matthew, you'll need to let Reverend Kumil in the house to work on our water heater on Wednesday."

Up until that point of summer vacation, Josh and I had avoided Dick by relying on the front door of the Staples' house. Dick's backyard remained as festive as ever, but now his friends were Christians wearing thin khakis and golf shirts instead of beer addicts in tank tops and flip-flops. They fried up hamburgers and hotdogs on the grill just like before, but to Amy Grant and Bible trivia games instead of KISS and horseshoes. Coke instead of Old Milwaukee.

"Did you hear me, Matthew? The water heater has been going bad for a while now, and he said he'd come up and take a look at it for us. He shouldn't get here before noon, so you can sleep to your usual time. Just make sure he takes his shoes off when he comes in."

"Are you serious, Mom? A dirty reverend?"

"Very funny. Yes, he'll still track mud all over the house on his way down to the basement. I'll make a thing of tuna salad so you can offer him a sandwich after he finishes. If you don't, he's liable to poke his head into the refrigerator and start griming things up."

"Why can't you just have him come on a Saturday when you're here?"

Mom giggles. "Well, Matthew, because I really believe he's the man who can get you going to church again."

A fist pounds relentlessly on the front door Wednesday morning. I raise my head off the pillow—the bedside clock reads a quarter to eleven. I jump from bed and scurry down the hallway shirtless and barefoot. Through the window I see it's Dick rapping away, his face skyward. I fiddle with the knob through sleepy eyes, his knuckles still tapping as fast as a woodpecker.

"Hey there, kid. Just came to work on your water heater."

"Yeah, sure. Come on in. Mom says to please take your shoes off."

"She at the office, is she?"

"Yeah."

Dick sets his sack of tools down in the entryway. "They're just work boots. I'll wipe real good and it'll be fine."

I rub my eyes and yawn. "Christ Wins" is on Dick's discolored shirt under his denim jacket. The extra layer of clothing isn't holding off his underarm stench any.

"How's things at Marshall, Josh?"

"Fine," I say, wondering how many times a man can forget names.

"Wearing you out by the looks of things." He chuckles. "I'm taking a course now at ABC myself."

"ABC?"

"Appalachian Bible College."

"Ah, right."

"Biblical knowledge. You know, spiritual nuts and bolts."

"Uh-huh."

Dick walks past me down the hallway toward the basement. His old khaki pants look like he's worked job after job in them for months without a wash: a collection of marks and stains as good as any in an art class.

"Don't you need your tools?" I ask as we enter the kitchen.

Dick stops and takes a look around. "Something smells good in here."

"I don't know what it would be, Dick."

"Give me a chance and I'll find it," he says straight-faced. "But, yeah, I probably do need them tools. Go ahead and carry them down. I might need you to show me a light switch or something anyway." I go back to retrieve the bag. "Don't know if you've heard, Josh, but I've been called by the Lord to preach. Matter of fact, tell your folks I'm preaching at Tucker Tabernacle tonight out Blue Creek. You all ought to come. Especially you since your mother tells me you ain't too interested in church no more. You kids always think you've got something better to do."

"I'll let them know," I say, flicking on a switch to the stairwell as Dick starts to head down. "By the way, how long you think this'll take, Dick?"

"Oh, shouldn't be more than half an hour to forty-five minutes I wouldn't think. Could be a lot less depending on what the problem is."

"All right, well I'll make sure you can find everything. Then I'm going to wash up and fix me a bowl of cereal. I was asleep until you knocked."

"I don't even wanna know, Josh," he says with a laugh as we cross to the utility room. Piles of junk fill the area, and shelves are packed with old toys and bags of clothes, but Dick finds the light switch and circuit breaker panel like it's his own home. He walks to the far corner of the room where the water heater is hidden behind boxes of Christmas decorations. I follow him and set the tools down as he bends over to check a valve, giving me another look at his rear valley.

"I'm gonna head on up," I say after a couple of minutes. "Give me a holler if you need anything."

"Oh, okay. Everything under control." I make it to the door before he adds, "Don't guess your mother's got any of her good tuna salad ready, does she?"

"Yeah, as a matter of fact she does. Soon as I wash and eat my breakfast, I'll make you a sandwich."

"Sounds fair to me."

Twenty minutes later, just as I'm finishing up my bowl of shredded wheat, Dick comes upstairs.

"All done except for the tuna salad," he says.

"Ah, right. Let me make you a sandwich."

"And a Coke or two will be fine."

Dick sits down at the table as I drop my empty glass and bowl in the sink, then pull a plate from the overhead cabinet. "Everything all right downstairs?" I ask as I reach into the refrigerator.

"Oh yeah. No big problem. I just had to adjust things a little, tighten things up in a few places, add a new...ah, well, no point in going into details you wouldn't understand. Your mother told me you're studying psychology or something, and science and engineering are a lot more complicated than all that. Anyway, here's a little something for you."

I look back as Dick places a large, laminated bookmark on the table.

"You've got your own Bible, don't you, Josh?"

"I'm sure I do somewhere," I reply, slapping a thick portion of tuna salad between two slices of white bread.

"Stick this in it. A little bit of utility for the Lord."

I cut the sandwich in half and open the fridge again to grab a can of Coke. "All right, Dick. Here you go. Sorry we don't have any hot dogs to go with that." I set the food and drink down in front of him and pick up the bookmark—might as well be a business card. In the center it reads: Reverend Dick Kumil—Pastor, Preacher, Prayer Warrior. Second Chronicles, 7:1 reads right below a picture of Dick and his family.

Dick takes a large bite of the sandwich. "I wish you had toasted it, but boy that's good, Josh. And by the way, it's kind of funny, ain't it?"

"What is?"

"Well, I'm fixing your water heater today and preaching on the fiery furnace tonight. You know all about old Shashrach, Medrach, and Abedneko, don't you?" Dick takes a swig of Coke that ends with a sound of satisfaction and small burp.

"Oh, sure. They're kind of like tuna salad, aren't they? Staple food."

Dick laughs and takes another bite. "I don't really know what you mean there, but I can tell you I've got a couple of twists for that church tonight. Gonna have them wonder what it'd be like if it were their three sons in that furnace."

"Wow. That's kind of like adding some habaneros to the tuna salad."

"Some what?"

"Hot peppers. Scorching. Kind of like a college exercise."

"You bet it is. And if you think about it, we're all headed into the fiery furnace unless we ask the Lord Jesus to save us. Don't matter how young you are, how prosperous or famous. Just look at them three fellows. I mean, you could be a king, you could be Rob Cruise or Bill Clinton. Don't matter."

I take Dick's bookmark and put it on the telephone stand behind him, wondering if anyone will ever use it. "Save it for Sunday night, Dick. Enjoy your sandwich now."

"You're right, son. Jesus don't wish indigestion on nobody."

"What time did your father get in from the library?" Mom asks when she returns home that evening from her secretarial job at Columbia Gas.

"Probably half an hour ago."

She sits down on the new, mauve sofa in the living room and takes off her heels. "Did he say anything about having to work at the book sale during the fourth of July weekend?"

"Nope. Nothing. He looked pooped and didn't say much. Kind of pissed off actually."

"Matthew. I've told you to clean up that mouth. This isn't your dorm hall."

"Sorry, Mom."

"Well, your father was having a rough day at work when I called him at lunchtime. It's harder than you think taking care of people all day."

"Yeah, it's kind of weird they call it a circulation desk and all Dad does is sit there all day. I bet his blood just stops moving after a while."

Mom stands up and walks slowly toward the kitchen with a slight limp. "And Dick showed up? Everything okay with that?"

"Yeah, I guess so. He left you a bill and a dirty plate. And as much hot air as hot water."

"Good. That's one less thing to worry about. You okay with tuna salad sandwiches tonight or do you want me to fix you some pasta?"

"Nah, tuna's fine, Mom."

"I'm going to eat one myself and then go clean up a bit for prayer meeting. Go ask your father if he wants one or two sandwiches."

I walk down the hallway and poke my nose in my parents' bedroom. Dad's in his adjacent bathroom with the door open.

"What did you say, Matt? I'm on the commode."

"Yeah, I know you're on the commode. Mom wants to know how many sandwiches you want."

"What kind of sandwiches?"

"Tuna salad."

"Oh, in that case better make it two. Tell her I'll be right in as soon as I'm out of the shower."

"That's what I figured," Mom says when I go back to the kitchen and relay the information. She's finished half her sandwich and takes another large bite, then gets up to make Dad's.

"Don't worry about mine, Mom. I'll make it myself once you all are gone."

"You sure, Matthew? Won't take me but a…" Mom stops and hunches her neck. "What in the world was that noise? Sounded like your father's dropped something big in there. Go and check on him, Matthew. I hope he didn't fall."

But before I can get up, Dad's tramping down the hallway. He comes in the kitchen dripping with water, wearing nothing but a bright yellow towel around his waist. He's breathing hard, and had no time for his patented comb-over. Without a word, he heads for the stairs and goes down to the basement, tiny puddles of water forming on the linoleum floor behind him. A sizeable welt has appeared on his shoulder blade.

"I thought Dick Kumil came out here to fix the water heater today?" he says when returning a few minutes later.

"Yes, honey. Matthew said he was here."

"You mean Reverend Kumil, Dad?"

"Yeah, whatever. I just got in the shower and scorched my back. Somebody better call him back out here before one of us roasts ourselves. That water's scalding and the temperature dial on the tank only reads 110."

"Honey, didn't you test the temperature of the water before you got in?"

"No, I didn't test it! I had the cold water on and turned the hot water to the same place I always turn it. He's screwed up somewhere. Matter of fact, what's his number? I'm calling him myself. I'm tired of shoddy work."

"Now, Tom, calm yourself down before you call him."

"I'm fine, Laura. What's the number?"

"Well let me go see if I can find it. I'll get you a shirt too."

"Don't worry, Mom. His number's here on a bookmark he gave me today." I smile and pick the card up from the telephone stand. "I meant to tell you Dick also invited us to Tucker Tabernacle tonight. He's preaching there on the three young men thrown into the fiery furnace."

"Matthew, be careful. Your father's about to burst a gasket."

"I'm serious. I'm not making that up."

Dad shakes his head and takes the card, searches for the telephone number. "Fiery furnace, my rear end." He finds the Bible verse instead. "Now when Solomon had made an end of praying, the fire came down from heaven, and consumed the burnt offering and the sacrifices; and the glory of the Lord filled the house."

"The number's on the back, Dad."

"What a nut. I'll show him a burnt offering."

"Tom, you're overreacting."

"Laura, I've told you before I don't know why you let him in this house after the things we've heard about his drinking. Matt, was he showing his ass-crack again today?"

"Yeah."

"You see, Laura? Well, I tell you what. He better get up here and show some more of it."

"Tom, that's enough."

Dad turns the bookmark over, marches over to the phone and dials.

Danny answers. "No, Daddy ain't in right now. Everybody went to prayer meeting to hear Daddy preach. I stayed home 'cause I've had a temperature since yesterday. It's almost 100."

Dad shakes his head in disgust. "About like your father's IQ. Now you listen, son. You have your daddy call Tom Wheedle when he gets in tonight, you hear? Tell him he left us with a fiery furnace this afternoon, and Shadrach, Meshach, and Abednego don't live here."

Dad slams down the phone. "For Pete's sake, he's already gone to church. We've got scalding water until tomorrow at least, thanks to that redeemed butthole."

Mom puts her head in her hands. It's not often we see Dad this enraged.

Dad tightens his towel around his waist. "Laura, I can't go to church like this. Used the bathroom and now a man can't even wash back *there*."

"Well I'll just stay home too then. People would ask where you are, and I'm not in the right frame of mind either."

Dad hovers over the table and eats one of his sandwiches, then leaves the kitchen. "I'll have heartburn now." He stays in his bedroom for the rest of the night with the television volume cranked high—war documentaries instead of the usual baseball games.

I turn the television on in the sitting room as well for *Billy the Exterminator* reruns. Two hours later the telephone rings. I pick it up on the first ring as Mom instructed so that Dad won't receive the call in the bedroom.

"Good evening. Wheedle residence."

"Is this Greg?"

"Sure."

"Greg, this is Reverend Kumil returning your call. I'm also wondering how come you all didn't come out tonight. Boy it got heated there. My sermon really fired up the congregation. I guess you all just went ahead to your regular church instead?"

"No, my parents didn't go to church tonight. And I never go anyway."

"Boy, they better get you into church. Whoremongers ain't the only ones that'll get the lake of fire. And let me tell you, hell don't burn sweet like that Coca-Cola either."

"Well, you drank our last can this afternoon, so I couldn't say."

Dick starts in again, and I hold the phone away from my ear as Mom walks toward me from the kitchen sink. She takes the phone from my hand.

"Good evening, Dick," she says as I take off for Dad's bedroom, hoping his fuse is still lit.

By Warlock's Design

Face stern and arms extended in front of himself like a sleepwalker, the warlock inched forward in the small room filled with smoke. Like a fool, I lit another smoke bomb and tossed it along the ground. Garrett, our fierce warlock, started coughing.

Fifteen minutes earlier, Garrett, Abe, and I were driving up and down hollows for a third straight Saturday, searching for a place to film our next scene. "This place is perfect," Abe shouted when we saw the two-storied, derelict, wooden shack set back off the road on a piece of accessible land up Barrens Creek Run. We scouted the building, then ran back to Abe's station wagon to carry our filming equipment, costumes, and props to the deteriorating cabin.

"All right, let's just get this over with," Garrett whined as he threw on his costume: a black robe we purchased for a dollar at Goodwill, a grey, long-haired wig that Mrs. Crumlin our biology teacher donated to the project, and unused sunlamp goggles we took from my brother's bedroom.

"So let's do this," I said. "Garrett, find the darkest corner in the building and turn on your inner warlock."

Abe set the camera on its tripod and we did a quick rehearsal. Then I lit the first three smoke bombs and Abe clicked the camera's red button.

Speaking in some thickly accented, creepy voice we had practiced for two weeks, Garrett even remembered his lines for once—interspersed with coughing. "Who dares tread on my territory, this sanctuary? Bow down to my dominion or depart this station at once, lest you desire actions that treat unbelievers of their maladies."

Abe signaled he'd zoomed out and locked the camera in a still position, then rushed to join me in the scene of two naive fellows searching for a missing friend. Running across the room he unexpectedly cracked open a rotten floorboard. I masked my giggle as his left foot disappeared through the hole. Professionals would have cut filming, but with no one manning the camera our usual one-take-and-done kept rolling.

The accident added to our ridiculous plot, and with Abe's foot stuck, Garrett started to play it by ear, moving beside my friend and thanking him for falling into one of his traps. Using the skinny Wiffle ball bat we had wrapped in duct tape to look like a lead pipe, Garrett attacked Abe's legs, back, and chest with blow after blow as our plot drifted into unplanned territory. I followed with my own new moves: rude names flew from my mouth to try and distract the warlock from beating my buddy to death. When the warlock turned his attention to me, Abe crawled out of the scene and picked up the video camera in time to film Garrett chasing me up the stairs. A busted window on the second floor gave me the escape needed to end our scene. Without a second thought I jumped. "I'll get you next time," the warlock shrieked, shaking a fist out the window under a now-lopsided wig. Outside I rolled around on the ground holding my ankle.

Five minutes later, filming finished, Abe and I laughed as we gathered our materials up to leave the property. Garrett mostly sulked while taking off his costume.

"Don't worry," Abe told me while returning to our car. "We'll edit out the rough stuff, add some Black Sabbath music, and everything will turn out even more grand than anticipated."

We had placed our tripod in the back of the station wagon, ready to leave, when two Ford trucks and an old Toyota Camry pulled up behind us. Five men stepped out of the vehicles, two carrying bolt-action rifles and two holding back slobbering German Shepherds. The fifth fellow, his face like a squirrel's, smoked a cigarette and did the talking from under his Marlboro cap.

"You boys better get the hell out of here right now or you're going to find these dogs' jaws around your ass! Don't know who you think you are, but you're nothing that can't go six feet under."

One of the other gun-toting, pot-bellied men in jeans and holey t-shirt agreed. He looked tense three weeks before deer season. The remaining three men only stared, one of them tucking away his Mail Pouch after adding a plug.

Garrett is naive and Abe's direct, so I quickly replied before one of them could say we were "just making a film." "We don't mean no trouble, and we'll get out of your way. Just looking for a place to light up."

"All that equipment's for lighting up, son?"

"No, no. That's just some stuff we're driving over to the Institute for my father to deliver to my uncle. He teaches film at State."

"Listen up. We see your scrawny faces again and you'll be going in a state institute yourself. We pull triggers on trespassers."

"Yes, sir," I said, signaling to Abe and Garrett with a nod toward the car. One of the men with a German Shepherd had started walking through the high grass to the abandoned house. I casually opened the car door—we needed to be gone before he reached the evidence of our smoky wizardry.

"Don't 'sir' me, you piece of shit. If we see you again a loaded nozzle will be up your skinny ass."

We jumped in the car and Abe turned on the engine. I told him to step on it with some urgency, and he shot out of the gravel and down the road in the wrong direction, leaving the men in a cloud of chalky dust.

"Hope we don't get stuck behind a coal truck," I said. "We've got about a minute before he finds our smoke bombs."

But the men didn't follow us, and half an hour later we replayed our footage at Abe's house, not mentioning the incident to his folks. "Wow. This is some of the best footage we've got so far!" Abe said. "Way worth the risk."

Garrett sat drinking lemonade with a scowl, unimpressed. "Yeah, but now I smell like moth balls and plastic from wearing that shitty costume. You always give me the crap roles."

Abe and I chuckled but didn't deny it. For our third, yet-to-be-titled film, we played the parts of two young men, the main characters, and left Garrett to play all the minor roles—from pregnant woman to warlock to dungeon prisoner. On most Saturdays when we filmed, we smoothed him over with bologna and mustard sandwiches on white bread and let him choose the tunes for the rest of the evening.

After a dinner of fried potatoes and ham, we sat at the dinner table talking about school and the rest of our film. Near midnight we ate cornflakes with added spoons of sugar and then headed into the basement to sleep. Abe jumped into his bed while Garrett and I rolled out some old sleeping bags that Abe kept in his attic. Garrett complained again about "stinky smells" while Abe and I giggled in the dark, imagining his sourpuss face. After another hour of laughs, we fell asleep.

We slept through Mrs. Detter's breakfast as usual, but could hear Abe's parents rummaging around upstairs as they got ready for church the next morning. Only then did I remember the deal I had made with my parents—too late now. Each Sunday, my folks, like the Detters, went to church services and then ate at Shoney's, not returning home until half past one.

After almost twelve hours in a thick sleeping bag, I got up pasted in sweat and grime, ate some more cornflakes, and got ready to head home for a shower. Only Abe had a license, so he drove both of us, dropping Garrett off first.

Mom and Dad sat in the family room, staring at me as soon as I walked into the house as if they had been waiting for me for days.

"So you didn't show up," Dad said without greeting me.

"You promised, Andrew. That's the deal we made," Mom continued, as if Dad had slapped her hand in a tag-team match. "You could spend Saturday night at Abe's as long as you made it to church this morning. All you had to do was go with the Detters. Honestly, we thought you were mature enough."

I didn't answer.

"What was the point then of taking your dress attire and loafers?" Dad asked.

I had forgotten about the ugly clothes since going to Abe's Saturday morning, and even forgot to bring them back home. "We couldn't really go since Garrett was with us, Dad. Abe stayed home, too," I said.

"Garrett Garcia? He's a nice boy. You should have brought him along," Mom countered.

"He's Filipino, Mom."

"And Filipinos can't go to church?"

"I thought he was Spanish," Dad said.

"Well, I never saw anyone like him come to our church," I answered.

"Honey, they're probably Catholic," Dad added.

"And his father's an engineer for Flat Top," I threw in. "Or maybe a lawyer."

"That's it, Andrew. You won't be staying over at Abe's on any more Saturday nights. I'm sorry, but I thought you responsible enough."

"Mrs. Detter said we could sleep in," I continued, making one final, weak attempt without showing frustration.

"Our deal wasn't with Mrs. Detter, son," Dad said. "We'll be looking at this problem a little more closely as a result." I knew that was code for a lot of lectures and a long grounding.

I raised my voice. "I'm not even saved. Why do I have to go every Sunday?"

"Two wrongs don't make a right," Mom replied. "You'd get saved if you had any sense, but it won't happen if you skip Sunday services. You'll go this evening and to Wednesday night prayer meeting to make it up. And you won't miss any more Sunday services as long as you live under this roof."

I turned away and walked back out the front door, slamming it behind me. Even my interest in showering had vanished.

"Now you come back here right now or else you'll be punished worse," Dad said.

Church deacons don't have any rifles or slobbering dogs, and I swore I wouldn't go to church that night or ever again.

I walked down the hill into the old coal town where I was born, a town that probably felt like I did, a town where I worried I'd live my whole life, a town that I doubted many people knew existed, stuck between two rivers and plenty of mountains. With little bottomland, town planners chiseled out the narrowest of places. Only a few of our old brick buildings rose more than two or three stories, but once in town they eclipsed any view of the surrounding mountains. A mall with chain stores had opened up a year earlier on the highway bypassing us, accelerating our slow but sure death.

Depending on who ask, John, Robert, and Ted Kennedy all visited us in 1960 and stayed at our little turn-of-the century hotel on separate occasions, but I could never imagine any President walking down the cracked sidewalks. When the hotel burned down last year, only coal miners renting rooms by the week complained.

Mr. Calhoun's Sweet Shack on Lewis Street stayed open until five on Sundays. As the only new business in town, I went there whenever I had a few dollars. Mr. Calhoun always said "business is delicious," but with few customers, I figured the store would probably close soon. The Sweet Shack sold only premium ice cream and made over forty flavors of milkshakes, but Dairy Queen had lowered their prices and offered new specials every week to make it even harder on him.

I stepped inside to the store's calm, dimmed lights and fans spinning on high. The Canterbury family sat at a front table. They greeted me and said Daniel had gone on a 4-H retreat for the weekend. Off to the side, an out-of-town coal manager sat by himself.

I selected a booth in the back where Patty brought me a menu. I already knew what I wanted: a pile of fries and a double-sized, chocolate peanut butter shake. While she placed my order I walked up to the counter for a pen and scrap paper. Tired of dwelling on my parents, I wanted to work out the rest of the plot for our film. Mr. Canterbury dropped some coins on the table that spun like game pieces as his family departed.

Patty brought my fries in minutes. I added ketchup and tossed the slim potatoes in my mouth two at a time as I began jotting down a few ideas that Garrett, Abe, and I had already mentioned. When the milkshake arrived, I tasted a spoonful of its chilly fat and both the fries and our script lost appeal. I took a few quick jabs with the spoon, then switched to a straw.

With my head hanging over the glass, staring at the table, I established a sipping rhythm, sucking the shake's sweetness up through the thin tube. And the weekend recreated itself: the old man's gritty, stained teeth as he shouted at me, Garrett's cough as we started to record, the coldness of the derelict cabin, Abe's yelps as Garrett hit him with the Wiffle ball bat. I didn't even hear Patty when she checked to see if I needed anything. The church service also arrived: hymns, testimonies, and the preaching I'd heard my entire life.

The Sweet Shop's door opened again and on cue Pastor Skaggs himself entered with his wife. He wore his trademark, midnight blue suit and sunglasses, his gray hair gelled and combed back.

"Hi there, Andrew. I see you didn't save any of that shake for me."

"Sorry."

Pastor Skaggs chuckled. "Say, listen, we missed you at church this morning. Feeling all right?"

"I'm fine."

"Talked to your mom and dad and they were sort of concerned. Hey, anytime you're in that situation, just bring your friends with you. We're all of the same family in Christ."

"Well, my friend Garret is Filipino," I said. Pastor Skaggs lowered his brow. "He's Catholic, too, I think."

"And who says we couldn't fix that?" Pastor Skaggs replied. "Never know unless we try, right?"

"We were busy making our film. We're trying to finish it before school's out. Graduation is soon."

"Hey, life's a balancing act? We have to find a way to make all the pieces fit together, but you can't leave out the most important piece. Just think about doing a puzzle and you leave one of those pieces out since you figured there was no time for it. Then, when you've finished your puzzle corner to corner and top to bottom, everything looks beautiful. Except there's one piece missing right in the middle. The heart of the puzzle. The lighthouse. So, you've built this nice landscape that looks all pretty, but no you're not safe and you're not content because you've forgotten the lighthouse. That's how it is with Jesus, too, if you forget him."

My face reddened.

"I realize that's probably a little over your head right now, Andrew, but you'll understand with time. Just remember you get to church every Sunday morning and evening. It's that simple." He paused. "Anyway, sounds like you're itching to be a movie star or something? You want into acting, script writing, or directing? You know there's no jobs around here in any of those categories. Most of them are out in that den of sin called Hollywood."

I never had any ideas of joining the movie industry or moving to California. I only wanted to make a cheap, amateur film with my friends about some monsters, mostly to get away a little bit from the ones I lived with every day and to swap boredom for a little adventure. "Thanks, Pastor Skaggs," I said, hoping he'd leave.

But he didn't go away. He kept talking even though I no longer heard what he said. I looked him in the eyes, looked deeply into the wrinkly cracks in his face and the oversized pores on his nose: another warlock in a dark, lonesome building, trapping me in his pew. Smoke formed and rose from the floor, and I knew that outside, in the heat of the day, the old, squirrelly-faced man and his team paced with guns and dogs.

WHEN WE SETTLE

"It'll probably just bring us out at Birch Run Road," Jimmy Paine whines, the hand-me-down flannel shirt tight on his plump frame. "Your boots are a lot better than mine, you know. My socks are already wet."

I urge him on, tell him we won't know without seeing for ourselves. "Besides, you got anything better to do?"

It's our first talk since leaving the gravel road and wandering into the woods behind the lumberyard. The dirt path ended at old tires lying around a rusty, door-less refrigerator in the weeds, so for a good half-mile we've walked through the underbrush, picking ticks off our legs and shoulders while listening to the trickle of the nearby creek. The buzz of traffic has faded, making it easy to forget the highway running on the narrow valley's shoulder, easy to imagine we are deep in the forest.

"Let's turn around," Jimmy says, his voice soft as he tries to hide his heavy breathing. "If we come out on the other side of the ridge we'll still have to walk another mile or more back home."

I know he's about done, know he hasn't liked it since the valley narrowed and turned our level walk into a slope through thick beech and elm. But just as he says it I see an opening in the trees ten yards ahead. Jimmy bursts forward. I can't catch up with him until he stops at the edge of a clearing, hands on hips, mouth open.

Two acres of bottomland are in front of us, picture-perfect, level as a plate on a table. A log cabin stands on the distant side of the land, the mountains rising sharply behind it. The creek on our left meanders to follow the cut of the land, slides past a small mill at the corner of the property, then runs up to the side of the house and heads into the hills.

Jimmy isn't interested in the postcard scenery. He catches his breath and shoots for the front door of the cabin. "Looks like olden days," he says, running past a collapsed outhouse and small well sealed up with concrete.

On the porch Jimmy tests several loose boards with his foot, finds a couple of places where the wood has rotted. The cabin itself looks habitable, almost cared for except for the foot-high grass tickling its foundation and the black tarp covering the front windows. Jimmy reaches for the knob of the front door and it falls loose in his hand. He presses his body against the entrance and strains. The door doesn't budge.

I walk to the side of the house. A foot above my head is a single window, its glass dusty. "Help me find some flat rocks and start stacking them," I call to Jimmy.

Within minutes I'm standing on a wobbly pile of stones. I push up on the bottom of the window. It doesn't open smoothly, but it's unlocked and I force a three-inch crack. I pull myself up, shift my weigh to the sill, and push the window open until it's wide enough to insert my head and neck. I push up with my shoulders to open it further, worming my body into the house before trying to cushion the fall with my hands. Jimmy quickly follows. Never worried about bruises, he dives in headfirst, then licks a sore that reopens on the side of his hand.

The dank smell of rainy woods hangs inside the three-roomed house. A thick layer of dust covers the simple furniture. In the kitchen a tin box rests on a dinner table pushed against the wall, and a cast iron kettle sits on the fireplace's cooking andiron. Empty earthenware and glass jars fill an overhead shelf, and cast iron pots hang from hooks in the wall.

"Don't bother looking for a light switch," I say. "There never was any."

"Black snakes don't need any light," Jimmy replies, his eyes wide as he follows me into the main room where a wooden table, dresser, and chairs are neatly arranged. He opens the dresser drawer and the smell of mold rushes out. "If nobody lives here, I can promise you they're in one of these corners."

"Maybe somebody is living here. Maybe someone from the lumberyard," I say while exploring.

"Well, it's neater than my bedroom. That's for sure," Jimmy answers, still opening drawers.

Neither of us sees the black and white photographs hanging on the wall in the main room until our third walk-through. Two of the photos are portraits, one of a man, the other a woman. Above them hangs a third, larger picture with three generations of people posing alongside a pair of horses.

"How old are these pictures?" Jimmy asks when I point them out.

"Who knows?" I answer, moving within a few inches of the photos as Jimmy's interest moves elsewhere. The man looks about forty years old and wears a light shirt under a buttoned, dark vest. Above his thin neck, cheekbones stick out under tiny brown eyes. He's clean-shaven with dark hair parted on the side. His small mouth is tensed as he stares into the camera.

The woman is dressed in a white blouse, a line of frills down the front. Her dark hair is piled high, and a subtle smile shows hesitancy. There are no backgrounds or color in the old portraits, giving them the strange power of another time.

The third photograph shows the man and woman standing in a group of eight people on the porch of the house. An elderly man with a cane holds his hat at his side. Two other women wear lacy dresses, one holding a baby wrapped in a blanket. Two children stand barefoot, one boy and one girl, their hands held by the women. Two horses are tied to a nearby wooden post.

"Hey, there's a rifle here leaning in the corner," Jimmy says, breaking my stare. He examines its every hole and crevice, explaining it's a flintlock musket with the name Booth written on its lock.

I'm more interested in the pictures. I look at them again and wonder what happened to the lives of the family. Are their bones resting in the ground around us? And how did these photos change the current of the air and put a wormy feeling on my skin? What sent my hand to fiddle in the space between the photograph and the wall?

From the crevice behind the man's portrait I pull out a worn, brown paper folded once down the middle, tiny cursive writing on both sides. I push my face down to it, struggling to read its sharp slant.

"I was born out of wedlock in Amherst County and so I took my mother's surname. My father's surname became my middle name, but it's been reduced to an initial now. Then Mother died…"

"What are you boys doing in here?" a shaky voice interrupts. I know it isn't Jimmy's.

I look up from the letter and find an old man pointing a rifle at us, his grey beard long and flowing like a waterfall. Overalls are strapped over his scrawny, shirtless chest. He's barefoot and has a wandering eye. His voice is weak and sickly, and even his firmest declaration lacks power. But a loaded gun still makes us the vulnerable ones. Jimmy puts the Booth on the ground, and I lower my hands, drop the paper. I glance at the old man's hand, the one with a finger on the trigger, and see the gnarled roots of work.

The old man's eyes say we shouldn't be there, that he's got a castle to defend. But then he sees the letter that has fallen from my hand. His jaws start to move like he's chewing gristle. He looks at me more intently and examines my clothes, puzzled by the dark green sweatshirt, jeans, baseball cap, and hiking boots. Then he lowers the gun and drops his head.

Jimmy stands quietly, and I can't speak.

The old man raises his head, nostrils flared and lips clenched. His eyes go to the photos on the wall. The faces in the pictures look even lonelier.

"Son, could you pick that letter up and read it to me? I don't know what it says." I reach down and pick up the old paper. I start reading again, this time out loud.

"I was born out of wedlock in Amherst County and so I took my mother's surname. My father's surname became my middle name, but it's been reduced to an initial now. Then Mother died when I was a teenager and the people said, 'Move on, son. You're hardy-boned enough and plenty hard-headed.' I figured a farmhand here is a farmhand there. I was born in backcountry and I'll die in backcountry. I figured on the other side of the mountains no one would know I was illegitimate."

I stop and look up. Even Jimmy is listening. The old man is staring at the floor. I am speaking more carefully than when reading in school, moving slowly to pronounce each word clearly.

"Things have turned out fine over those hills. My first wife passed, but hard fought I have my own family, my own property here, my own horses and own gun. Right at the foot of our mountain is a little creek gurgling and bubbling, babbling like a child, reminding me where I came from. We've planted and we've grown, feeding sweetly off the land. The tobacco plants of

Virginia are forgotten. So are the boats loaded with all they could handle, sent down a rough James River to Lynchburg.

"There were plenty of stops before I made it here, plenty of people I worked for, both good and bad. Plenty of work, and my back took the worst of it, but that is not as bad as this talk of war. What more should a man want but an opportunity to work green fields that'll produce something for himself and his family? And now that my children have moved to other lands, now that their mother has departed, it is time to prepare my own bed.

"This nation grows large and grand. The guns are more powerful. Railroad tracks have opened the forests and rivers. But we would be mad to forget that the land we toil is for our family, our community. For every hand, every leg, every lung comes from the land. We can neither trade, nor buy, the mysteries of the soil.

"I write this knowing, yes, it too will burn or fade or blow away, but I write with the faith that took me over the mountain. Should I believe I have cared for them? No, they have cared for me. So humbly I sign, Clarence Coleman Given."

I lower the paper to a silent room.

Then the old man speaks. "Son, could you read it to me again?"

So I start from the beginning, read it twice more. I know the old man is memorizing the words. For once Jimmy isn't fidgeting. He's quieter than he's ever been in church and school.

"No more," the man says after the third read, the words pocketed in his mind. He takes a deep breath and wipes his brow with the back of his hand. "I thank you." He pauses. "Go ahead and put that letter back behind the picture where you found it, son. Then you boys follow me. Bring that musket if you want," he says to Jimmy. "It's yours now."

I fold the paper and carefully place it behind the photograph while Jimmy picks up the musket. The old man turns and leaves with surprising energy. We follow him outside where he's started up the creek, farther into the mountains. I look to Jimmy, but he's already in pursuit. We don't catch up with the old man until he reaches a knob on the ridge where he sits down and pats the ground beside him in invitation.

Jimmy accepts first, putting some space between him and the old man. I sit down between them and we look out at the opposite ridge, sliced in half to put in the highway. The sky is cloudy and grey, and in the distance the little cars zip by without a sound. On a spot down below us we make out the edge of an old cemetery clearing.

"That's where Clarence Coleman Given rests," the old man says as he points. I lean over for a better view. "You boys ought to pay him a visit some time."

"Down there in the valley there were ten or twelve homesteads surrounded by cornfields," the old man continues. "Green beans. Onions. Cabbage. You name it. And up in these hills were deer, rabbit, pheasant, and turkey. Don't think it was like those little gardens now. Or that there were separate deer seasons for bows and guns."

"Now take a look out at that highway. Look closely and don't accept the first thing you see or hear."

I squint to make the distant automobiles clearer, studying the highway as instructed. Jimmy and the old man are quiet, looking out as well. But the longer I stare the more the highway's dull pavement glistens, turns to bright silver and starts to run in watery waves. The cars begin to streak by less frequently, then hardly at all. The few that pass seem to float by like boats over the steady flow of a river. I am lost in it.

When Jimmy nudges me some time later, I look around for the old man, but he's gone. "You ready to go?" Jimmy asks.

I nod and Jimmy stands up and leads the way back down the mountain. We don't speak. In less than an hour we're back at his house where we wash off and sit down on the sofa with Cokes. Jimmy turns the television on, but for once neither of us cares to watch.

I've walked to the lumberyard many times since that day two decades ago. It's changed little, and the small trailer still sits rusted and vacant on the back corner of the grounds. In twenty years I've never seen anyone working the site even though the trees in the hills behind it grow thinner and thinner. Each time I go I stare at the fallen oaks and maples, the stacks of lumber, realizing that even as a boy I felt something illicit hanging around those grounds, something ghostly.

I never told Jimmy, but the day after we met the old man, I returned alone to the woods. I walked along the creek to the bottomland where we found the log cabin, but there was no house, no well, no old man. I still stop to look each time I return there, thinking if I linger that it all might reappear. Sometimes I continue on up the mountain to watch the cars flying by on the highway, and sometimes I visit the tiny cemetery on the ridge, Clarence Coleman Given's name wearing away on a faded tombstone.

Jimmy never went back with me. He doesn't even talk about that day. But in a corner of his parents' garage, behind rusty rakes and cobwebbed tennis racquets, sits the old man's musket. Booth still readable across its lock, it now collects a different dust.

ABOUT THE AUTHOR

Timothy Dodd was born and raised in Mink Shoals, WV. He earned his B.A. in comparative religion at Wesleyan University in Middletown, CT, and is completing his MFA in creative writing at the University of Texas El Paso. Currently he works as a public school, ESL teacher in Philadelphia, PA.

Also a poet, his poems have appeared in many literary magazines including *The Literary Review*, *Modern Poetry Quarterly Review*, and *Broad River Review*. His interview, "Life & Death & Poetry", can be read online at the *Roanoke Review*. He is currently looking for a publisher for his first collection of poems entitled *Modern Ancient*, while putting together a second collection of Appalachian poetry.

As a visual artist, Tim had his first exhibition, *Secondhand Smoke*, in Manila, Philippines' Mono8 Gallery in 2018. His solo show, *Come Here, Nervousness* appeared at Manila's Art Underground gallery in July 2019. His expressionistic oil paintings can be seen at various other group exhibitions and galleries, as can a sample of his art on his Instagram page *@timothybdoddartwork*.

Tim naturally enjoys returning to his roots in West Virginia, as well as traveling and living abroad in such countries as the Republic of Georgia, Chile, and Zimbabwe. A passionate music lover, he delves neurotically into many forms of music, from 80s New wave to Senegalese mbalax and various subgenres of heavy metal, particularly from Finland and Iceland.

In addition to the stories in this book, he has had fiction published in *Yemassee*, *Glassworks Magazine*, *Kudzu*, *Noctua Review*, and elsewhere. *Fissures* is his first full-length collection and portrait of contemporary Appalachia.